The Paris-Napoli Express

Janice Kulyk Keefer

"The Paris-Napoli Express" was first published in *PRISM International* and won first prize in the *PRISM International* Fiction Competition, 1984. "The Dream of Eve" originally appeared in *Antigonish Review*. "Viper's Bugloss" was first published in *Quarry* and "Somewhere in Italy" first appeared in *Malahat Review*. "Red River Cruise" was first published in *NeWest Review* and "Mrs. Mucharski and the Princess" was originally published in *Atlantis*. "In a Dream" first appeared in *Canadian Fiction Magazine*. "Mrs. Putnam at the Planetarium" won first prize in the 1985 CBC Radio Literary Competition and was originally published in *Radio Guide*.

ISBN 0 88750 623 2 (hardcover)
ISBN 0 88750 624 0 (softcover)

Cover art by Egon Schiele
Book design by Michael Macklem

Printed in Canada

PUBLISHED IN CANADA BY OBERON PRESS

For my parents, Joseph and Natalie Kulyk

The Paris-Napoli Express

Jerry was still belching champagne and dreaming of Sheba when they entered the Gare de Lyon. He knew that his legs were moving and that Teddy had the valise. And he also knew in some tight corner of his brain that if he weren't to arrive in Marseilles on time Sheba would have left him forever, or rather, let him go, like a tennis ball that has lost its bounce. So he was visibly, palpably grateful to Teddy for carrying the valise and wrestling directions and information from the seedy porters, and furious that the sod had gotten him drunk over petits-fours when he'd known how crucial this arrival in Marseilles would be. All during his stay Jerry had talked of nothing else: in cafés, galleries and lecture halls, in the gardens of the Palais Royal, under the portico of the Madeleine and in front of every one of the manifold crucifixions and martyrdoms in the museums he'd talked of Sheba, almost in defence against this pressure of culture and Catholicism that weighed on him as heavily as the pastry and the custard cream from that obsessive tea. And Teddy hadn't stopped him—much: Teddy was acquainted with Sheba, in fact they may even have been lovers once, when Paris had been new to Sheba and she'd needed the right sort of apartment in which to stay. Teddy was in Le Marais, in a seventeenth-century *hôtel particulier* that had not been tarted up by any inflated Iranian heiress. It would have been Sheba's type of place at the time: almost certainly they had been lovers.

There were two high steps up; to steady himself Jerry focused on the little placard stapled to the side of the car: Paris-Napoli Express. He was sober enough to know that he wanted one saying "Paris-Lyon-and-whatever-after"; he had to make the connection at Lyon. "Sure, sure," he seemed to hear Teddy saying in a voice as dearly comforting as old Tokay: "Look, Jerry, I'll double-check for you." He left him in a compartment that seemed evacuated: it was late Sunday afternoon and there should have been a million provincials going home. Instead there was but one tall, long-haired, back-packed young girl who nodded at him as if in apology for something and then returned to stitching up her bedroll. Teddy was gone—no, he could see him out the window, questioning someone who was leaning out of a neighbouring train that bore the placard Paris-Lyon-Basle. That was the train he wanted—good, kind Ted to have made sure. He tried to stand up to grab his bag from the luggage rack but slipped sideways so that he was reclining, one knee archly pointed, across the sofa-seat. That girl will think I'm piss-drunk, he thought; to make a gesture of sobriety he asked her the time in what turned out a metallic falsetto—his voice always rose two octaves when he drank champagne. She flushed and shook her head: was he so incomprehensible, was his speech so slurred? What would she be thinking? And where was that traitor, that Jesus, that weaseling creep: oh, here, Teddy, grasping his elbow when he'd offered a hand. "So long, love to Sheba, don't forget the connection at Lyon—only a couple of minutes, so get your gear into the corridor a good ten minutes before the train pulls in. No, nothing to worry about—the other train leaves an hour later, same route: if you want to meet Sheba on time it will have to be this one. Good luck, old man: been a pleasure— see what I can do for you this side—love to Sheba—tell her Gunther Gonzales is the man to get in touch with if he's still in Caracas. Ciao!" And Teddy was gone.

He managed to swing his legs down and slump into the space of one seat, closing his eyes so that he wouldn't see the other train across the rails. If there was one thing he hated and feared it was a contagion of possibility: there was only one train he wanted, only one, that other was a snare and a delusion: no delusion but real enough—he would wait it out, he would endure. In ten minutes the wheels would roll, he would close his eyes and sleep, wrestling with a dreamed anxiety rather than the everyday terrors of railway compartments, whistling porters, indecipherable large print upon window-ledges and over doors. His mouth was dry; he had to piss—he let his eyelids rattle down and dozed in steep discomfort. Jerry dreamt in cinematic genres and this might have been early Hitchcock. The shy hiker was hatted and veiled, a Madeleine Carroll; there were border police, an espionage ring among the ticket collectors, hints of war in the jolting headlines of another passenger's newspaper. Sheba did not figure, unless perhaps as the director.

"Reservato, reservato, vedere!" The French inspector did not want to see his papers but a tall Italian woman was pushing something over his nose: the dream swelled and then broke entirely, leaving him only the hard fact that he had to get up and find a toilet. He nodded to the seven others who seemed to have filled the compartment while he'd lain sleeping, and he stumbled over some feet and sacks of groceries as he made his way into the corridor. By this time the train had started—too late, too late to jump out and make triply sure: here he was, stuck with his valise and the galley-proofs he had been sent to collect by Sheba. But Teddy had made sure. He found the toilet. Buttoning up he felt suddenly, masterfully sober: he knew exactly how to find his way back to the compartment and this time he could decipher the instructions and prohibitions posted through the train: "E pericoloso...." Italian, the train was Italian and going to Italy! Yes, but stopping at Lyon: three hours or so and then he'd get off and more Italians would get on: admirable simplicity, order, coherence—the woman leaning over him, the tongue-tied girl—wonderful sense it made to him, now. He would try out his seven pages of phrase-book banalities on them both, it would help to pass the time. The corridors were crowded: luggage, slouching conversationalists, those little fold-down seats that latecomers have to angle upon, shifting and turning every time someone comes by. Jerry apologized to a man on one of these seats as he opened the door to his compartment and ended by sitting next to him on an even narrower seat some three minutes later. Reservato, reservato: the lady, imperially slicing some provalone, had made that clear: yes, there was an extra place but not for the signore; her cousin would be returning, returning: reservato. Jerry turned and looked for the tall, sallow girl with the bedroll: she was gone. His thoughts began to loll again—Teddy and that fucking champagne; why hadn't they come earlier and reserved a seat? There was a special formula for bribing porters, Teddy must have known, might have told him—he would be dead by the time he reached Marseilles, sitting like this. You didn't make excuses to Sheba. It would be midnight by the time he reached her—she would insist on talking shop, too.

He had the galleys in his valise and he sat there on the fold-out seat with the valise in his lap like some heavy sleepy child whom he daren't wake lest it begin to scream. He couldn't expect her to be on the platform or even at the gate; she would be correcting copy in the station restaurant—you could not miss her, even sitting down. No hat—her hair long, thick, that peculiarly fine dead-brown like oak leaves in the fall. In black, probably, or else smack in red: shoes, bag, coat. With her glasses, which she would take off deliberately the moment he reached the table, not out of any irrepressible vanity but because she was saving her eyes for her work—nobody knew how Sheba could read so much with only one pair of eyes and astigmatism, too. Her one physical weakness she wore like a defiance, making you feel that it was you and not her eyeballs that were askew and distorted. Jerry began to wonder just how much more of a mess he could appear to her without her glasses—his every hair an anarchist, his mouth uneven, clothes threatening a breach of promise with his body, even his voice a stutter he'd corrected into a slur. How had she ever? With him, Sheba ...Teddy hadn't believed it, he was almost sure. But what should he care—after all, he and not Teddy would be in Marseilles with Sheba before the day was over.

Jerry twisted on his seat to watch how rapidly the countryside was passing by. The factories and towns had long since disappeared and there was only a quick monotony of darkening grass and a cold sky in which the moon was just beginning to take form. The moon, the same moon, he reminded himself, that would be shining in Montreal, in Marseilles and in Jerusalem, whether he met Sheba or not. In Jerusalem, he repeated to himself, half-expecting that ripening blank to turn red in the night sky by the magic of old words and expectation. It stayed the same: it was like looking into an eye from which pupil and iris had vanished, leaving a null white. He veered his head from the window,

9

swivelled round and happened—that enormous valise on his knees—to knock from his neighbour's hands the book he was somehow reading in that jolting corridor. Jerry nearly gutted himself on the suitcase handle, bending down to retrieve the book: "Scuse, scuse," he kept repeating, even though the title of the book was *The Letters of Lord Byron:* even though the man was saying, "Not at all; thank you ever so much," in an accent as confident as it was fastidious. The man seemed to want to talk—at any rate he took advantage of Jerry's embarrassment to begin his address:

"You are not English. Well, to be English is not everything—though I sometimes think it is everything that matters. My mother was English, though she lived all her married life in Florence. Oh, yes, even the war years: you can imagine how dreadful that was for her. My mother gave me my English. She read Byron to me when I was just a small boy. I owe her everything. You are not English—Canadian, then? There's no need for gratified surprise, I am not one of those stupid Europeans who conceive every foreigner to be an American. They—they are the danger, as everyone knows—"

He was a bore, but thankfully one of those bores to whom one needn't pay the compliment of appearing to listen. Jerry just looked at the man: conservatively dressed in old but excellent clothing; tie-pin, vest, summer tweeds; gold-rimmed spectacles on a round but unjovial face; long and exquisitely curved hands that seemed to grow out of the ancient binding of the Byron. An impoverished, upper-class Italian—or why would he be sitting here, unless he had quarrelled with his travelling companions in one of the compartments? He was talking irrepressibly, despite the competition (someone a few feet down from them was reading the trilingual safety precautions posted over the emergency door—first in Italian, then in fast and florid French, finally in German, a deliberately hysterical Nazi-German). Jerry felt stiff and sore and uneasy and the man never stopped....

"—regrettably those so vital currents in the soul of the English people were not tapped: the wrong men in power, fools. Everyone knows that Sir Winston's mother was an American, and the Americans have always been controlled by unwholesome elements within—"

Jerry stood up to let a fat woman in a tracksuit get by. "Prego, prego," she beamed at him, the words a loud, sweet kiss on his ears. He watched her disappear into the compartment; as she opened the curtained door a winy gust of laughter blew toward him. Everyone on this train seemed to know one another, everyone but he must be going to Naples. He checked his watch—another hour to Lyon, then a dash to the platform from which the southern train would depart. Sheba would still be with Proctor at his villa outside Arles: incredible contacts, had Sheba. She'd persuaded the great man to write a series of articles for one of the periodicals she was co-editing: it was a coup, it would make her name, except that she'd already made it. The one name it might make would be his, Jerry's. Sheba had liked an article he'd written in *Northern Soil,* and invited him to write for her own, much more important review. And now, to be collaborating with her and Proctor—his reputation would be secured, he would be safe and sound, a bona-fide wiseman; he would also have Sheba. She had been amazingly honest with him when they'd first begun seeing each other; she'd said, "At this point, I admire you, Jerry—and I only sleep with people I admire. And I can see that you're the kind who lives with someone, so you might as well come and stay with me, for as long as my admiration lasts. And that, Jerry, is entirely up to you."

Whether she was admiring Proctor now, he couldn't guess: Sheba didn't just go after names—witness him, Jerry. But then she'd confessed a deliberate weakness to Jerry: she wanted a child, she would have a child and so for the last month they had slept without pills, diaphragm or condoms. It had been as rigorous as if they were using all

11

three precautions at once, and Jerry couldn't help thinking of Sheba's last lover, warning, as he'd cleared his socks and underwear out of the dresser that would become Jerry's, that where most women had a uterus, Sheba had an extra cranium. Sour grapes, that—he could understand, though. But Jerry was still in a position of strength; she would have to be waiting for him, especially since he didn't have the address of Proctor's villa, nor the temerity to track them down. She'd sent him an ultimatum via Teddy's Telex machine: "Meet Marseilles, last train Sunday. Proctoring. Busy! Sheba." But it was a sure thing, sure as rain, as railway timetables: Teddy had looked them up and told him he could take his time. They had gone for a stroll to the Ile de la Cité on Sunday morning and boozed it up over a lunch so late Teddy had called it tea. Teddy was English—the English were simply the finest people in the world....

"—and not only the finest, but the purest, the strongest. An island race, uncontaminated by—"

"Scuse, scuse, signore." The compartment door directly in front of him was opening: not the fat lady, but a child. There was a howl of laughter at something the boy was saying—Jerry wondered what sort of a joke an eight-year-old could be making to provoke that sensuous laughter, redolent of garlic sausage and Lacrimae Christi. Would he have time to grab a crocque-monsieur at the Lyon station? God he was lonely—hungry, he meant. The boy seemed to have heard his thoughts, for he shoved a hunk of sausage under Jerry's nose and the whole compartment choked on its amusement. Jerry was about to push the kid away until he noticed that this was no child but a dwarf, and probably a good five years his senior. He froze and the laughter burst again, even more raucous and filling. The man on the seat beside him gave a sharp kick to the dwarf's groin, but it had been anticipated: the dwarf leapt back into the compartment and somehow among all the legs and picnic refuse found place to perform a perfect little goose-step, his eyes straight on Jerry's neighbour who kept silence until the dance ended and then said six or seven words in an Italian not to be discovered in *Friendship Phrasebooks*. No-one said a word until the fat lady poked her head into the corridor from the compartment in which she'd been sitting. She jumped out and billowed down the aisle, came to the dwarf and, plucking up imaginary skirts, curtseyed and kissed his forehead. He, in his turn, spread out his arms and making a bright cushion of the woman's pliant belly, cradled his head there, burlesquing the bliss of a stupid child. Then, joining hands, the two bowed to the compartment and the corridor. Jerry's neighbour had gone; someone poured a cup of wine for the performers and invited them to join the party. It was decided, however, to take their show from room to room—they had bundled out and were going down the corridor when the woman gestured to that same compartment in which Teddy had first abandoned him. The same dictatorial lady was there, but it seemed as if the cousin had never showed up. Before Jerry knew what was happening he'd a hunk of bread and a paper cup full of some very sweet, brownish-looking wine in his hands. "Veni, veni, mange signore!" was what they seemed to be saying. Was he hungry, did he have time? He could feel his belly rollicking along the rails in its sudden emptiness; he would just toss this down and his bags into the corridor and be gone—surely Sheba couldn't begrudge him this?

"Non Inglese, non Americano—si, si, Canadese: bene, grazie," was all he managed in reply to their questions. They kept refilling his paper cup—a jolly man with hairy hands and an abstract-patterned sports shirt was encouraging him to drink up. For the first time he looked around the compartment: the jolly sports shirt, the aristocratic lady with the provalone and the absent cousin, a nice old woman crocheting rapidly, her hands knotting, twisting, pulling, with all the certainty and skill of a hangman fashioning a noose and all the time her eyes on his face, dark, no, black eyes, slightly raised at the corners, as if they were doing the friendly work for her lips, which stayed in their tight straight line. And last, two teenagers playing cards together, oblivious of his presence—were they brother and sister or just look-alikes, or was he seeing double? His cup was filled again and again—everyone except the card-players was watching him, expecting something: the silence was so complete he could hear the breadcrumbs sticking sharply in his throat. Were they Mafiosi—had they Mont-real connections, perhaps? Or was there some definite sympathy now with that gentleman in the corridor—was this a trap, was he still dreaming: espionage, war, trains, Europe .... He rose, suddenly, to run: the train swerved and sent the wine he still clutched in his hands down over his trousers, in a sticky-sweet parody of his fears. How, oh how could he ever escape—and how could he meet Sheba looking like this?

The train jerked sideways and sent him flying into the grandmother's lap: he threw his arms around her to steady himself and managed to put his left hand through her piece of crocheting. Her skin smelled of lavender, her blouse of starch, her hands of the stiff dustiness of her lace. She smelled like his own mother—and with her strong, tilting eyes upon him he settled back into his proper place like an excitable, chastened schoolboy. What was happening to him? All that he wanted was to secure his happiness, to make his little success in life—was that so immoderate a desire, were these such obvious lies? Even as he shut his eyes, wishing himself out of this compartment, out of the window—pergolesi? pericoloso; non e permesso—even as he told himself it was only five more minutes to Lyon, he knew. The very speed of the train was shouting it to him, it would not be stopping anywhere, except for Napoli. He groaned and opened his eyes only in time to see the station at Lyon whirring past: on one of its tracks a sister train, Paris-Lyon-Basle, letting its passengers leisurely out—or was he imagining things? Teddy, that bastard, had screwed him—he must have known—he knew Sheba at any rate, and that would be good enough. What had he opened along with that magnum of champagne: jealousy, pathos? A mistake—in the proofs? Or a mistake to be going like that to wherever Sheba was snapping her fingers? "What's in it for you, Jerry-old-man; she's not your type, and even if she were she wouldn't deserve you. You're decent, is what you are—a man of feeling—a man of fearing—a man of here's your train, don't forget the connection at Lyon—only a couple of minutes...."

Or was he, Jerry, fabricating all this, now? She'd never wait for him—he'd be in Naples this morning and she'd have left Arles, Proctor, be flying back to Toronto, telling her cleaning woman to pack up his gear and send it off to St.-Vincent de Paul, so that he'd have nothing once he got back. Back, when, how—Sheba had the money, the tickets: surely she'd leave them for him at the Canadian consulate in Marseilles? Why had he left home in the first place? Because she'd told him to—that brainy bitch, that intellectual houri, that Sheba—and he thinking he could play a mock-up Solomon to her, coming here. Here, on this bitch of a continent, him! Born in Montreal, he'd never been further west than Toronto: those two cities were the safe poles of his earthly existence. He found the grandmother looking at him, her mouth drooping into pity. "My son, my son, what did I tell you—stick to your own, stay where it's safe"—but she only wrapped her lace around her hand, wriggled it into an even loop, and started over again. More wine—the stains on his trousers had dried—they must be near the border, now. At least he had his passport, but mightn't they still arrest him, eject him, imprison him?

Out the window darkness had thickened into night; the world was blackness and a rasp of moon—it frightened him, this void pastoral through which he and his plans and all his desires had come to speed. He tried to secure himself by thoughts of home, the True North, true in proportion as it was safe, sound, plush, easy. There were the tall glass office towers, reflecting only each other in their concrete parade down the dear, familiar streets: Yonge, Bay, Bloor, Spadina: the very words were a charm. Oh sweet, sweet new world where all Europeans were just immigrants and ethnics, their hates and loves and politics reduced to the dimensions of a little Italy, an Oktoberfest, storybook Baba Yagas instead of Babi Yars: the week before he'd come to Paris there'd been a synagogue bombed there—stick to your own sweet home, my son, your own home ground.... But all around him a tipple of Italian, gestures at him, to him, over him—the kids in the corner stopping their card game and reaching into the luggage rack, retrieving rolled pillows that they spread beneath their heads, falling asleep against each other.

Where was that fat woman and her dwarf, that ample mother and her constricted son? Sheba had been looking to her projected child: why not Proctor, why not Teddy, why him, grateful, scatty, pettily ambitious Jerry? Only because—prego, prego, scuse, vino—she would want a child she could manage, dictate to, edit like an effluviate manuscript: his child, a part of him—would she even own him as the father if she did conceive? And she on her way even now to the station at Marseilles, with someone's book on Hegel and another's on Macherey and a dozen reviews of the latest significant Canadian novels while he tumbled out without a lire into the nauseous dawn of a Neapolitan fishmarket. Up went his hands to his disordered head while he groaned aloud, "Sheba, Sheba, what have I let you do to me —to mine!"

His cry was like glass dropped upon ceramic tiles: slivers of true, petulant grief shot out into the ears of everyone, except for the two friends, heads together, fast asleep. He would be thought a madman—he had to speak to them, say something they would understand or he'd be thrown out, handed over to the border police, betrayed. Ransacking his brains for all the opera libretti he could remember he produced something at last: "Amore, amore: si, sposa mia: perfida, tradita: mia tragedia, Dio mio, tragedia mia!!!" The little man with the wine bottle made a sign for concerted silence: he corked up the bottle with a ceremonial flourish, as if he were concluding an aria. And then he stood, and stepped over to Jerry, who looked up into the man's eyes: black, big and profound lakes in which the whites flicked like fishes, and then blanks, perfectly null and distant, and then leather-hooded, with the look of circumambient hatred given by that fastidious fascist in the corridor. Silence or voices, Sheba, Teddy, the ticket inspector: first in a rolling and rich Italian, then in florid French, finally in a deliberate, hysterical German—he reached out for the little man to knock him over, to steady himself, but fell down instead and out the window, rolling, rolling, covered in glass and rich Italian.... The jolly man in the violently patterned sports shirt lifted him gently in his arms and pushed him back into his seat. He reached up for a pillow, lodged it under Jerry's lolling head, folded the arms across the chest, and left him to sleep.

Half an hour later there were visitors to the compartment: the little man gave a grunt, inclined his head to Jerry and murmured something about the drunken Canadese in their midst—"Amore: e pazzo." Then the fat lady in her scarlet tracksuit, so red that it gave even her sweat a febrile glow, turned to her companion. The dwarf winked at her; they began a little pantomime, Romeo e Giulietta, she peering down from the balcony of her bosom, he arching up from his knees, at which the audience began to laugh again, louder than ever, while Jerry snored in the relief of dreams. At last the big, red Juliet bent down in a grotesquely amorous pose; kissed the dwarf on his retreating forehead and then, with a shove of her hips, knocked him down flat to the jolting floor. The laughter was by now uproarious: the ticket collectors and border officials who were climbing into the train had rushed to the compartment and caught the last of the tragedy. Wine was poured out and offered around: tickets were flashed and passports dangled; healths drunk, news exchanged and Jerry dozed through it all, hidden under baskets and blankets and the bulk of the entertainers. The officials moved on, scattering laughter behind them. One by one the compartments extinguished their lights as their occupants settled down for sleep, sweaters draped over shoulders, provisions neatly basketed, heads rolling together, blinds drawn upon that night whose lights shone out serene as a straight line, with a purpose all their own, and only incidentally illumining the rails on which the Paris-Napoli express sped its way home.

At Windy Cove

Just from the way the bell rang, Griet knew who'd come into the store. Customers—the local fishermen, builders of the new wharf or the older women from the outskirts of the village—pushed right in and slammed the door behind them, so that the bell bawled out its signal. Kids trying to shoplift a bag of chips or a handful of jawbreakers had a way of lifting the door up against its hinges, so that the bell was half-throttled in its warning. But only Sunny could produce that small, snuffed ring that sounded for all the world like a bleating lamb in the damp dusk of a winter's night.

By the time Griet hung the dishcloth on the rack, tucked her shirt-tails back into her jeans and came downstairs into the store, Sunny was settled in at the counter, tracing x's and o's with her long fingers over the glass jars stuffed with peppermints and double bubble gum in slightly frayed wrappers—Griet and Eric bought them secondhand from a wholesaler in Digby. She twirled round on her stool as Griet clunked through the bead curtain, and offered her face the way other people would a hand, by way of greeting.

You noticed first the fluffy bell of hair Griet would have called mouse-brown, if Sunny hadn't at their very first meeting told her it was ash—"Blonde sandray-ay," she'd said. Then the soft, almost muddied features: grey eyes, a little quiver of a nose and a mouth both small and full, inclined to purse up at whoever spoke to her, signalling resistance stubborn as it was silly. Griet figured Vince had the shape of that mouth stubbed into his skin by now: Vince was Sunny's husband, he'd practically grown up in Windy Cove with Griet and Eric and right now he was upstairs putting in a new kitchen, for which they were paying him mostly in groceries. He'd been at work a month now, and that made it two weeks that Sunny had half-pushed, half-persuaded open the door of the Dutch Variety, to sit at the counter and talk while Griet took inventory or polished the worst of the summer's smudges off the candy jars and coolers.

The first time Sunny had waited to be seated: she'd held out her hand to Griet and introduced herself as Mrs. Vincent Stubbs. She'd been dressed in a skirt and sweater like a model in one of those magazines Griet sold, but never had time to read; the sweater was pink angora, the skirt grey wool, and both had the same vague softness of Sunny's face and voice. Her shoes were soft, too—suede, with hardly a rubbed spot on them. She'd stood with her back against the door she hadn't quite shut behind her—Griet had felt a long whistle of autumn wind right through her until she'd moved Sunny aside and shut the door herself.

"It doesn't ring when you do it," Sunny said.

"Of course not," Griet had answered. "What would be the use of that?"

Sunny had looked up from under lashes so long it seemed her eyes would trip over them, as if to confess that she'd never understand about the bell or anything else, from why there were so many different streaks of blue in the sea on a windy day, to what she was doing here in the first place. And then she'd said, "Is my husband here?" as if she were asking for the explanation of some law of physics. Griet had followed through with the demonstration, taking Sunny by the hand, through the bead curtain and up concrete steps into the house.

Down a hallway patterned with blowsy roses Vince could be seen in his workman's overalls, with a tape measure and carpenter's square in his pockets, just like an illustration from a Grade 3 Primer on "Work Men Do." When he saw them he dropped his tools, wiped his face with the palm of his hand and strode down the hallway, the coarse material of his overalls making a whistling noise between his legs. He slapped Griet's shoulder—he didn't touch Sunny, except with his smile—and said how glad he was that Sunny'd come and introduced herself like he'd been telling her to since the day they arrived. She didn't know anyone here— anyone in the whole East, he'd emphasized—she'd never travelled more than a hundred miles from her hometown all her life, and home was in Alberta. He didn't even mention the name of the town—nor did Sunny. It was as if a name would rob them of the outrageous distance they had come, that he had put between Sunny and her mother. All Griet found out until the very end, was that from the main street you could look up and see mountains, and that the most water all in one place Sunny'd seen before coming to Nova Scotia had been a creek that dried up each July, so all you could do was paddle your feet in it and look for minnows.

So that was how Sunny started coming round to the Dutch Variety, sometimes trying to help out by flicking the feather duster Griet had never been able to sell, or by straightening the rows of canned beans and peaches and pilchards, most often just sitting on the stool by the counter, stroking smooth her stockings or tinkling her charm bracelet, and making confession to Griet. She was like a small child pouring herself a glass of water from a brimming pitcher— things came splashing down over the sides, all in a puddle, so that Griet had more than the whole village could have ever wanted to know.

It was because Griet's face was the way it was: perfectly round and strong and open; dependable as an earthenware mug full of strong, hot coffee. Or because of the way her brown hair parted down the middle with the exactitude of a national highway; because of her voice, which had a slight phlegmatic tone, and her face that had the stolid ruddiness that decks the plainness of people in old Dutch paintings. People told her things—the tourists who came all summer long to buy sliced bread and strawberry jam and the instant coffee that always had an after-taste of mushroom soup, would begin to gabble as they counted their change, first about where they'd come from and how crowded the campsite was; and then about how their wives picked holidays to get all bitchy with period cramps, or how their husbands couldn't stuff their beer bellies fast enough into their bathing trunks so they could get down to the beach and set themselves to broil before the little sluts parading near-naked on the sand. Even the dignified ones who rented the old white houses overlooking the bay would start to complain about what a crime it was to be putting in that new wharf, all that steel and cement, when the old pilings were so pretty and suited the character of Windy Cove, and didn't she agree? Griet would stare with her perfectly round eyes in her perfectly round face and say, "It's not character that keeps us fed in winter, after all you folks go home." And the tourists had understood, just from the set of Griet's face, how they were mere ghosts in nylon wind-jackets and pastel-coloured rubber boots to the fishermen and construction workers who lunged into the Dutch Variety November through to May for bolts and nails and three kinds of fluorescent-orange twine; for Coca-Cola and the ersatz-pastrami sandwiches Griet heated up in the microwave she kept like a little tabernacle on the shelf behind the counter.

Sunny was probably more of a ghost to these men than any tourist from Maine or Ohio or Southern Ontario. Griet remembered how once, soon after Sunny had started coming round, the engineer supervising the construction of the new wharf had come in for some cigarettes and a new lighter. Steve Deveau: over from Moncton he was. Sunny had been at the baked goods, reaching up on tiptoe to straighten the cake mixes so the labels on the packages would show perfectly symmetrical. The bell had startled her—she'd knocked one of the boxes down, whirled round and crouched as tidy as a cat, Griet thought, to get it, and, still crouching, had looked up at them. Sunny didn't blush, but just went paler under the spots of rouge she'd pressed along her cheekbones; then she shook out her hair, exactly like a soft, mute bell, and smiled. Deveau didn't bend down to help her retrieve the packet—he didn't smile back at her or say a word. But Griet remembered how he hadn't taken his black, narrowed eyes off Sunny's body until she'd risen, dusted off the packet, shrugged her narrow shoulders at Griet and walked over to the garbage can, into which she dropped the cake mix. By the time she turned round, Deveau had gone —without a word, just as if she'd been a ghost.

Sunny had gone home right after that. As soon as she was alone, Griet had hurried to the garbage (it was a fresh bag she'd just put in that morning), fished out the packet, and returned it—Angel Confetti Cake—to the shelf from which it had fallen.

Later, Griet would wonder what the truth was about Sunny —whether you could expect truth about anyone so helplessly contrary. Take her name, which made you think of bright yellow curtains on holiday mornings—and then look at her. She made you think, Griet's husband said, of a Persian cat—of the fur on a Persian cat's belly, all matted and dull and softer even than a baby's hair. Griet had looked hard at Eric when he'd said that—she didn't like the picture it made of an Eric she didn't know, sitting and stroking a breed of cat she'd only ever seen on a TV commercial for the expensive kind of cat food you can't buy in bulk. And she'd wondered—as she'd done every once in a while through her twelve years of marriage—about what Eric did with his time in Digby, and on the trucking jobs that took him up to Cape Breton or through New Brunswick, while she stayed behind to mind the kids and the store.

Sunny had never asked Griet about the kids—she'd hardly ever seen them. They were eight and ten, the age where they were always off at school or out at play or squirrelled up before the TV—so you could hardly expect Sunny to show an interest. The one person she did talk about was her mother—how pretty and gentle she was, and brave, too, ever since Sunny's father had died. And how she spent just about her every penny on Sunny, so she'd have good things to eat and nice things to wear—she was always knitting for her; look at this sweater—and Griet was called on to admire a mauve affair in mohair with stiff little knobs sprouting all over and making Sunny's breasts look even smaller and harder—like apples on a tree left to grow wild.

"My mother," Sunny went on, "she gave us the most thoughtful going-away present. It's a windchime made out of porcelain—there's a white dove at the top, and all sorts of little doves tied on strings underneath; it's just lovely. I got Vincent to hang it up on the porch as soon as we moved in; it makes the prettiest sound in the breeze. Except that there is no breeze around here, just that awful wind. Each time there's a storm more of the birds get broken off—I find bits of them in the grass around the porch—just like a broken china cup. I think it's a shame, Griet—that you can't have pretty things in a place like this." She slipped off the stool on which she'd been perched: black vinyl it was covered with, and there was a rip in it that Griet should have patched long ago; it had turned into a long, sharp slit with dirty-looking foam rubber pushing through.

"I don't know it's such a shame," Griet answered, her hands on her hips. "At least my folks thought this place was good enough for them. They came after the war, when I was six—from Holland."

"The war—?" Sunny quavered.

"Yeah. World War Two. I never got enough milk to drink until I came to Canada. My mother says her milk looked blue, it was so thin and poor—and I was lucky to get that. Me, I put both of mine on Similac straight away when it came my turn, and I advise you to do the same. I've got a whole shelf of the ready-mixed stuff, for mothers who come camping during the summer—do you want to see?"

Sunny shook her head violently; she looked as if she'd swallowed a safety-pin and was terrified it would open up inside her somewhere. "She can't be more than twenty," Griet suddenly thought, "and scared shitless about having a baby so far from home; probably grown up on old wives' tales about how if you think bad thoughts your kid'll be born with two heads or no fingers." She was about to say something reassuring when Sunny went on as if she hadn't heard anything Griet had said.

"Just a shame. That wind—at night sometimes you can hear the mirrors rattle on the walls—nothing's insulated, you just can't get warm."

Griet nodded and automatically plugged in the kettle on the counter, as if to warm Sunny's feelings with some coffee. Vince and Sunny were renting—or had for free, just the payment of half a year's property tax—the house of a widow who spent from October to June in a mobile home somewhere in Florida. It was one of those old, square, white places with a rising sun carved over the front door. Tourists —not the campers, but the other kind who stayed in The Olde Elme Inne and left copies of *Historic Nova Scotia* on their dashboards—were always stopping in front of that house and taking photographs to add to their pictures of trashy outhouses and rotting lobster traps. They used to take pictures of Griet's house, too—before she and Eric had torn down the front to put in the concrete box that became the Dutch Variety. There'd been all kinds of stupid fuss from the retired couples who owned summer houses in Windy Cove—most of them had refused to set foot inside the store and nine years later were still driving to Digby for their groceries. Griet was used to it by now—she figured that the fuss would die down when they died off, and that couldn't be long in coming. She took a package of peanut butter cookies from the shelf, put some on a plate and pushed them along with a styrofoam cup of coffee over to Sunny.

But Sunny didn't even notice. She was smoothing the pleats of her kilt and straightening the points of her collar where it surfaced over her mauve sweater. "He promised me we'd live like kings if we moved out east," she said. "And now"—she walked over to the mirror behind the counter —"now we haven't even enough money for me to call home when I want. It would cost almost a thousand dollars, he said, to fly me there and back. A thousand dollars we haven't got and never will."

She said all this simply, without whining, in the solemn way a child entrusts a secret. She was trying to fish her reflection from a pool of glass clotted with lotto tickets and expired coupons and the kids' school photographs. And to the mirror she confessed, "I hate it now, when we're together in bed. It's not the doing it—I just lie back and float through that, like one of those coloured buoys out in the harbour. It's what he leaves me with—the smell of it and the sting. Salt—it smells just like the sea."

Then Griet remembered the one time she'd convinced Sunny to take a walk with her down to the cove one early November afternoon. They'd taken the road that curved past the store and along a narrow river to the bluffs that overlooked the sea. They'd stood for a while where the tents of summer campers had once been pegged as thick as flies on those sticky coils that hang from the ceilings of restaurant kitchens. The tide was half out: the crescent of beach so pale it looked like ice crystals and not sand below. Then Griet had led the way down to the jetty, past the tar-papered outhouses and along the ramp to a strip of concrete against which enormous granite boulders had somehow been piled. Beyond them was the sea, its waves seeming to grate one upon another, its surface a crazy quilt of blues and greens and greys. Gulls were silently lording the boulders, so near to them they could have counted the feathers on their wings, or stroked the strident oranges and yellows of their bills and webbed feet. And the cold bright roughness of the time and the place had made Griet stretch out her arms and flap them absurdly at her sides, as if she were some great, ungainly gull about to glide into perfect airy grace.

Sunny had just stood there, noticing other things— things Griet would never have thought to look for, just as she didn't strain her eyes to see the crystals of salt that primed the wind. Sunny pointed to a heap of bleaching, bruise-coloured crabs around the shacks; to the rotting codfish dumped against the pilings of the jetty. It was too cold to smell them, that would come with spring, yet Sunny insisted that she could. "It—it stinks here," she forced out over the wind. "It stinks of salt and fish guts—and the sea. The air's thick with salt and slime—I hate it here. It's like we're on an island in the middle of the sea and can't get back to shore—"

"We're not on an island—it's just the way the coast

rounds back on itself—" Griet interrupted, but Sunny kept on shouting.

"—have to get back, I have to, I'll die here, I'll die—" And Sunny had stood shrieking, with her voice no louder in the wind than the whisper in a conch shell held up to your ear. The wind whipped the strands of her hair until they looked like snakes, with snakes' split tongues, and suddenly Griet was terrified the girl would be blown off the wharf over the boulders into the freezing stew of the sea. She'd grabbed Sunny's arm and tugged her back down the ramp, along the road to home. Once back in the store, Sunny at the counter, cradling a cup of hot chocolate between her reddened hands, Griet had laughed at herself for her foolishness—Sunny was all right, just nervy and finicky and a stranger still; Vince and time would cure all that. But now, as she watched Sunny's image in the mirror, she saw the same face she'd seen on the wharf that afternoon, the same muddied mask of panic and disgust.

Griet ran over to the mirror and fumbled with the cards cached inside its frame, breaking Sunny's reflection. The girl went back to the counter and began to drink the tepid coffee Griet had poured her, pressing her fingernails into the styrofoam when Griet asked, "Why don't you do something, then? Make some money of your own."

"What could I do here?"

"How the Jesus do I know what you can do? What can any woman do to earn a bit of pin money? Christ, you could knit, crochet—Christmas ornaments, for example. There's a shop across the bay in Yarmouth where all the tourists from the Boston states come over on the ferry in the summer. Shop sells nothing but crafts, Christmas stuff—you know, to hang on trees and doors and hooks, like. My mother-in-law keeps herself comfortable with the cash she makes off that—buys herself new lampshades from the catalogue, things like that."

Sunny frowned into the bottom of the cup. "I can't knit

—my mother, she does all that kind of thing so well I never wanted to try. And besides, I couldn't get nearly enough money—I'd rather do something with people, I mean." Sunny looked up suddenly with the kind of smile Griet remembered seeing on the faces of her own children when they had first learned, as babies, how powerful a mere gesture of their face could be. "Oh Griet," she said, "couldn't I work here—for you? I'd arrange things so pretty— people'd come in and take pictures of the shelves, they'd look so good. And I've got experience—I used to work after school as a check-out girl in the supermarket at home. Couldn't I, please—?"

Griet dumped the untouched cookies back into the bag, and shoved it into the cupboard over the sink. "Don't be stupid, Sunny; if I had any money to pay salaries, I'd start by paying my own. Or Eric, so he didn't have to go off moonlighting all the time. Oh for Christ's sake, don't cry—don't you even have a handkerchief—here's a napkin. Besides, we're paying what we can to Vince, aren't we—and paying him's like paying you. Don't take it so hard—just wait till summer—he's bound to get work then, with the summer folk coming back to their houses and needing their roofs reshingled or their window-sills replaced—those old places just sit there rotting all winter—should be a gold mine once people get smart and tear them down and put up new houses. 'Course, it was just like Vince to light out west just as everything was starting to cave in there, like some giant sand castle. I don't mean—Vince is a great guy, I mean, hard worker, and takes pride; you should see what he can do on a boat—"

"On a boat," Sunny repeated, dully. She slid off the stool, slipped her arms into her coat and adjusted her scarf around her neck, so that it reached up to the tips of her ears: they poked out the fluff of her hair like the scrolled, rosy shells that speckle the summer sands. Griet watched through the window as Sunny walked not up the hill to home, but

29

straight down the road to the new wharf, where the builders were at work, their hands blistering under the rubber gloves they bought by the dozen from Griet's store; where Mr. Deveau, the engineer, would be sitting inside his small, plastic-walled hut, smoking cigarettes and tapping his fingers against his thighs.

After that Sunny never came to the store—Vince apologized for her, saying she slept so badly nights—what with the wind, and her being so delicate she could never keep her hands or feet from freezing up, and it was his fault they couldn't afford to heat the house the way he'd like—that Sunny spent most of the day in bed: only got up to fix him supper in the evening. Griet was glad to hear that at least she could do that—all Vince ever brought in his lunchpail was a sandwich Griet would put into the microwave for him when he broke off work. But he never complained, he treated Sunny and Sunny's feelings as if they were bone china—Griet had watched him once reaching out to touch Sunny's arm with fingers that seemed to bleed tenderness from under the bruised nails. He'd be good with kids, too, Griet thought; not like Eric, who was always either tickling theirs into hysterics, or else giving them the back of his hand. And as for the way Eric was with her—well, maybe it was a good thing he was on the road so much—and yet she was a good wife, better than he deserved; if he'd just once touch her the way Vince had Sunny—who was no more solid use than a ball of slut's wool underneath a bed. Why Vince had had to tie that tin can onto his tail, she'd never know. And neither, she guessed, would he.

Griet's kids came down with whooping cough right after Christmas, and she closed up shop to look after them. She even sent Vince off for the month it took to get them back to rights. When he started up work again Griet was too tired to do much more than notice how thin he'd got, and hunched; how his eyes looked strained, like dogs at a chain from which they can't break free. Before she got her wits together to ask him any questions, Eric had come home from New Brunswick and picked up all the answers at the social club where he'd drunk half a dozen beers while Vince had cried over one. About how Sunny had packed up and gone —left all the wedding gifts it had cost an arm and a leg to bring from out west—the pots and pans and portable sewing machine—and taken only a suitcase with her clothes.

"Gone where—how?"

"To her mother, he figures—clear across the fucking country—kid's got clams in his head to bust up his guts over that—after what he told me—"

"What did he tell you, what?"

"Shit, all kinds of stuff—like she was so scared he'd get her pregnant she took the pill *and* squirted herself with that foam stuff each time he so much as fingered her—Christ, she musta looked like strawberry shortcake inside. And other stuff. But the Jeezus is he don't have a clue how she got the money to high-tail it home—"

"Maybe her mother sent it. Maybe she got lucky on a lottery ticket, maybe—"

"Maybe she was laying on tail for the whole construction crew at the new wharf—"

"Shut up, Eric, shut your filthy mouth up—how can you say that—she's a frigging baby. But you're bastards, all of you men—or fools, or both." And Griet sprang up from the sofa, switched off the TV and stomped off to bed, leaving Eric belching alone in front of the blind, bare screen.

One week later a letter came—for Griet—no-one else.

Well, I'm here—I've come home like I said I would. My mother just wept when she saw me at the door—just hugged me and wept, till my hair was about soaked through. I don't think she'll ever let me go so far away from home again.

Mother's thinking of selling the house and getting an apartment in Edmonton. She thinks I could get work in a department store there—Ladies Wear. I'd like that, I guess.

I hope you and Eric do fine with your store, Griet. I liked helping you. I think your house will be so pretty when it's finished—the kitchen and everything.

If Mr. Deveau should ever ask about me, tell him I made it safe and sound and will never, never be back.

So that's all, Griet, except—can I ask you a favour? It's something that's been bothering me ever since I got home—I even dream about it. That windchime I told you about—well, by the time I left, all those porcelain birds were gone—the wind smashed them, and there was nothing left except an ugly, stupid, knotted string hanging from the porch. Vincent tied it up for me there—with real strong knots—you'll need a kitchen knife to cut it down. Could you please, Griet—I don't like to think about it hanging empty like that, in the wind. Would you please, please get rid of it? That's all.

Love to the kids,
Sunny.

The Dream of Eve

She was working her way down to Vézelay—it was there she had arranged to do the greater part of her research. Autun was on the way—you couldn't pass through the south of Burgundy without stopping for at least an afternoon at Autun. For students of Romanesque architecture (and Mrs. Anderson was writing a thesis on the subject: why else had she left home to come to France this summer?) it is essential to stop off at Autun. Evelyn Anderson stopped and stayed five days.

She'd been in and out and around the cathedral every one

of those five days; she'd been twice to the Musée Rolin, where she'd made notes on Ghislebertus' carvings of St. Lazarus, Martha, Eve and Mary. She had taken her own photographs and purchased reproductions, capitalizing on the detour—for her own subject was Vézelay, and she was impatient to arrive there, settle her papers and get to work.

She had ten weeks in France on a university grant; they expected her to do impressive things—successful things, and she was confident she could. She had only to concentrate impressions, fix her responses the way scientists smear specimens onto glass slides and let them stiffen. Once back home she could recombine these separate elements into a complete experience of the sculpture and the buildings she had seen. People she would have time only to glance at; voices, to hear in a well-padded distance: she would make no friends this first time away, in Europe. So that when the abbé at Autun suggested she look up a certain Madame Riault who was translating an excellent treatise on the cathedral sculpture, she took the address, folded it into accordion pleats, and posted it into the pocket of her raincoat. This was exactly the sort of thing she didn't need or want—interruptions, salutations, postscripts—all she'd have time to scribble down would be ten short weeks of chiselled, hoisted stone. So that when it happened she was both annoyed and flustered, for the woman had proved charming, seductively enthused.

"Pardon, madame—je m'excuse—tous vos papiers—oh, you're American—you'll forgive me, Canadian, of course. Jesus Mary and Joseph, what a mess I've made careerin' into you like that. No, let me get them—one's blown into that corner now—watch out for the pigeon droppings, they don't wash out. What a hell of a lot of—"

It was like walking on turf that bounces up and down under the stoutest shoes. Mrs. Anderson let the woman talk on for the pleasure of hearing the sounds she made: she had no interest in either the apology or the rescue work. In fact, she was dissatisfied with the notes she'd made—she couldn't care less, at this moment, if they scattered over all the rooftops of Autun. It often turned out like that— knowing she couldn't work but writing anyway, ending up on a word jag, producing rubbish and trying to convince herself that it was worth the time she was wasting. This Irishwoman—and she couldn't have left County Kerry more than a week ago by the sound of her voice—seemed persuaded that she'd done her a real injury. What was worse, she'd only to glance at a few of the sheets she was handing over to realize who Mrs. Anderson was.

"Of course, sure and I'm an ass—you're the lady Father Prévost was tellin' me all about. I do feel awful—I've been flat on my back all week and haven't had the time to look up my own family, so you'll forgive me for not chasin' you down at your hotel. Which one did you get? Oh, the *Beau Séjour*—that's good—they'll treat you decently. But for how long are you in town? Leavin' tomorrow—oh, you can't! But listen, the least I can do now is take you home and give you a drink—stinkin' weather, isn't it, enough to grow moss on your bones. Look, you'll come and have a drink and we can talk about your work, and I'll maybe show you this bitch of a thing I'm translatin'—"

It was a miserable day: the old stones seemed to be spitting up the rain they'd lapped and there was nothing for it but the mildewed loneliness of the hotel or one of the museums she'd already exhausted. Mrs. Anderson was sick of writing up her notes and looking over manuscripts—she could do worse than spend an hour with a scatty Irishwoman. They found the car and Bridie started chattering again as soon as the engine had started up. Bridie—that really was her name, and she did look like Siobhan McKenna's younger sister, a pretty girl from County Kerry who was turning into a lovely older woman in Autun.

Bridie was saying that she'd met her husband—he taught English at the college on the outskirts of the town

—in Leeds, where she'd been training as a nurse, and he'd been studying English. This was well after the war—she'd been born just before the beginning of it—but then in Ireland that was no special trouble, it was like having the rest of the world join the family, when they all went to war. So she'd abandoned her training and come to live in Autun— heavenly town, but the Romans had made one calamitous mistake—right calamitous—in building it on a north-facing slope: fine for one of your sun-spotted Italian towns, but here.... And that's where she'd been for the last twenty years. Come without a word of French, but had picked it up and spoke it well enough now not to absolutely shame the kids. Bridie had three of them, all girls: one married—too young, having a baby already and not yet twenty—one still at home, and the oldest off at Trinity College, Dublin— marvellous place to be. Rosaleen, that was her oldest: but she was back in Autun for the summer break, she was staying with them.

"And you?" But the car had stopped in front of a sprawling house just outside the city, and they were out the doors and dodging clots of rain up a crooked walk so that Evelyn didn't have to answer, yet.

"Look, it's a holy mess, but you won't take any notice— you're a good soul, aren't you—a partner in crime." Bridie took her coat and hung it in the kitchen to dry; they went into the study, where the whisky was.

It was the kind of dry, distinctive mess that impresses rather than disgusts non-academics: toppling heaps of books and runaway papers, but flowers in porcelain vases and here and there a few delicately gilded, lyre-back chairs undeluged by print. Bridie opened a cabinet, calling out "Whisky—or will you have sherry? It's all we have, so you'll be stickin' your tongue into one or t'other." Mrs. Anderson deliberated as the glasses were being rinsed: if she asked for a whisky, what would Bridie think—it was only three in the afternoon. Thank god there hadn't been a word about tea so far.

She was dying for a whisky—and surely sherry was unthinkable in France? Perhaps Bridie had already sized her up and was offering sherry as a compassionate cover, to create a fiction of choice? Hell, she'd take the whisky and be damned. But somehow it came out as sherry, and she sat tilting the small glass in her hands as Bridie tossed off a shot of whisky, neat, and then screwed up the bottle. "Sweet Jesus, it's the only thing'll help a body these bad days," she sighed. The rain was still coming down in strings outside; the two women sank into a slightly damp sofa and before long Evelyn was telling Bridie "just a bit about herself."

There was no reason to lie, but then there was no point in spilling it all out to a stranger on the first go. She said the things she always said to people she would meet but once in her life. She was working on a master's thesis for the University of Manitoba, in Canada. Western Canada. She was staying at Vézelay for the summer—Autun was just a stop on the way. Yes, she was married: children too, of course—though they were all grown up now, so that she was free at last to do what she'd always wanted: to use her head a bit, get out of the house, clear right away from.... "But aren't these your own girls, here?" Evelyn switched, pointing to some photographs trapped under the glass of the coffee table. Three pictures of three girls, two of them pretty, one rather beautiful. And then some photos of an older couple with three or four small children in their arms. A nice, comforting-looking, middle-aged man and a dark-haired woman, holding all those kids. But the woman was Bridie —it was a rotten picture, didn't do her justice since she was good-looking, Bridie, and Evelyn thought that if you listened to her long enough you'd end by calling her beautiful. Yes, those three were her kids; the fellow over there that Mrs. Anderson had her finger on—that was her husband, Laurent. As for those other kids—weren't they incredible, though?

Bridie leaned over to a magazine rack, rummaged

through it, found what she wanted and put it into Evelyn's lap. *Catholic Life:* on the cover a fortyish couple surrounded by a dozen or more children, mostly Asiatic or African. Evelyn looked up flush into Bridie's face and saw for the first time the silver cross chained so precisely round her soft, white neck, as if Bridie were the rare and exquisite pet of some absent master. She closed her hands around her sherry glass and listened to Bridie's heaped explanations.

Wonderful people—friends of theirs—a couple without any means to speak of, who had adopted twenty kids in all: battered children from the town; dafties turned out of their homes by peasant parents who didn't know any better; even babies, mites with running sores literally sold to them for a packet of fags in Tangiers, Cairo, Singapore. This darlin' girl—in that photograph, over there—wasn't she a darlin' with her huge black eyes, and such tiny, fragile limbs—the mother had been savaging the girl when Gilles and Marie had come by. And had sold her, just like that—Bridie here snapped her long, ringed fingers. And the mother young, so young it had to have been her firstborn she was palming off.

"And she actually said to them this, something like this, 'Go on, take her, but let me know the day she kicks off at last; I'll have a fête, with all my friends.' What a fiend to say a thing like that before her own child—any child. But look at her now—happy, healthy, doesn't have nightmares any more, goes to school and is bright as a button! Would you believe the things that can be done to help people, if only we'd give ourselves up to doing them?"

Evelyn was shaking her head as if in wonder, rising to ask if she might call a cab—making polite excuses, citing a non-existent rendezvous, anything to get her out of this house in which all the virtues seemed to be niched like alabaster statuettes—when a girl whirled into the room, one of the girls in the photographs. You needed no qualifying adverbs: she was beautiful. And as she went up behind the sofa to her mother, kissing the top of her head and draping

38

her arms over her shoulders, she jumped out of the photograph into the very image of what her mother must have been 25 years ago. My Irish rose: Kathleen Mavourneen. But no, her name was Sylvaine and she came to shake hands with Mrs. Anderson in the tight, correct way that well-brought-up French children do. She was talking with a comic, charming pout to her lips of a party dress that she needed to buy. There was nothing whatsoever in the shops: *rien, rien, rien du tout*. Her mother laughed at the tragic finality she put into her "nothing," and then she said, "But you can speak English, darlin'—Mrs. Anderson does." And so Sylvaine broke into the same springy sing-song that her mother used, and with the two of them pattering on it could have been a duet, one of those shamrock and sugar-lump songs that used to get printed in "Popular Piano Pieces" of the forties. Except that these two were laughing at one another and ended up in French at Sylvaine's insistence until it was finally decided that she should borrow one of the dresses that her older sister had brought back from Dublin.

There was no more talk about the twenty orphan children; the magazine itself got buried under the proofs of Bridie's translation, which they hadn't even finished thumbing by the time the husband came home. Laurent was impeccable—he neither asked nor insisted that she stay to dinner, but merely announced that he would make for her such an *omelette aux fines herbes* as she would never taste in any of the restaurants of Autun. And instead of asking her preference he went straight to the old wardrobe in which the whisky was kept, and poured her out a tumblerful.

They ate in the kitchen—the dining-room table was still strewn with Bridie's translation. Over omelet and garden salad and bottles of strong Jurassien wine they talked. Again, Evelyn shook out the short, bleached sheet of who she was and what she did and then they tumbled into various things—a Buddhist lamasery that had opened in a nearby, half-ruined ch[a]teau; the Common Market; Quebec—and even St. Boniface. The wine was pungent and the kitchen windows steamy but Evelyn merely downed another glass —this was the kind of shirt-sleeves conversation—fast, fluent, forgettable—that she hadn't had since she'd left Canada weeks before.

The two girls joined in all the way through—there seemed to be an easy parity between parents and children; you could say what you liked and weren't to be hushed when you contradicted someone else's views. Sylvaine always agreed with her sister Rosaleen, who wasn't nearly as pretty, but was indomitably Irish-looking. Laurent called his daughters by private, pet names; his wife was always, "my love, sweetheart, my darling." And Bridie sat queening it in the drenched half-light of the kitchen, looking lavishly beautiful, finer, richer now than both her daughters put together: consummate. She was wearing one of those Indian cotton dresses, gathered at the yoke, full-sleeved and skirted, and a mist of dusky colours—purples, greens, blues. Her family teased her as she told familiar, yet perfectly funny stories about life in Dublin in the fifties.

Evelyn just looked at them all and then up to the walls, at the foxed prints and the saucepans clumped there. They did not ask her any more about herself or her ideas—they'd got hold now of some mutual sponge of interests and were letting it expand under their hands in a pool of indulgent attention. Evelyn didn't mind—she just sipped her wine and broke her bread into bits around her plate, watching the game of happy families play itself out across the table in the low, dewy light. When Laurent helped her on with her coat and she shook hands with them all, she said with some truth and a rather liquid warmth that she had enjoyed all this so much—meeting them, spending the afternoon and evening in their company, in their home. She promised to look for Bridie's book when it came out—and to look them up if ever she came back their way. And of course, should they ever find themselves in Manitoba....

In the car on the way back to the hotel, Laurent did the talking. About Bridie, mostly. "She's marvellous, just marvellous." There were no Irish bells in his words, only a Merseyside lurch. "One of a family of twelve; we go off to Ireland almost every year for our holidays. And she does so much—in the house, with the children, our friends, work in the community.... Bridie's good works—I couldn't begin to tell you. This thing about the babies—murdering helpless children—"

"Yes, she told me—the couple who've adopted ten or twenty orphans."

"No, the other thing—there was a girl in Sylvaine's lycée—conceived a child and before Bridie could even get to speak to her, she had to run off to one of those legalized butchers, and that was that. Baby tipped into the dustbin, along with broken bottles and cigarette butts. God, but I've seen my wife weep—here we are, *Le Beau Séjour*. You're sure you won't stay over in Autun another day—we'd love to see you again *chez nous*. You really must leave tomorrow morning? Well, then, all the best, cheerio!"

She overslept her train, waking late the next morning with her head pulped not just by the whisky and Jurassien wine but by the nightmare that had finally plucked her loose from matted sleep. Children with matchstick arms and legs and their mothers beating them, beating until the children caught fire and were consumed in a pitiful, rancid flame of suffering.

The next train left at four that afternoon. Not only had the *hotelier* not bothered calling her at seven that morning, he demanded that she leave her room as soon as possible. A flock of amateur archeologists was expected any moment for a three-day conference: every room they had would be required. And it was still raining, though not so heavily as the day before. Mrs. Anderson took a cab to the station, deposited her bags and sat down to a leathery croissant and a cup of black coffee in the station café. She'd been given sugar, but no spoon to stir it with. A crowd of uniformed schoolgirls suddenly rushed into the café, as bright and bumptious as balloons. Mrs. Anderson paid her bill, left the half-eaten croissant on the little metal table, and walked out the station doors into the town.

The slope of the streets was such that you couldn't help plunging into the cathedral square, no matter how many and how devious the turnings you took. What else was there to do but, as she had already done five days that week, stop on the cathedral steps in front of the tympanum and put the fingers of her eyes over the surfaces she knew by heart. Yet her eyes, this time, refused the whole—instead they focused on one small section that she'd never really seen before. Well below the Christ, a pair of hands, steely and locked as forceps, hauled one of the judged out of its foetal crouch. Impossible to tell whether they were angel's or demon's, those hands—whether the cowed, crouching shape was of the saved, or damned. Beside this foetus-shape was another, certainly damned—flames snaking its thighs; retching laughter at the sight of its neighbour's excision from that long, lodged row of naked prisoners. It may only have been the dregs of her nightmare but Mrs. Anderson knew suddenly that the damned, laughing creature had breasts, however skeletal—and that the figure being hugged by those blades of hands was the creature's child. But she could not judge, though she seemed to be skinning her eyes with her staring, whether the child were being raised to the Christ, or lowered back into its mother's company. Food for snakes, writhing, insatiable: Bridie— *Catholic Life*—a packet of fags.... Surely that woman had had some cause, selling her child like that; surely you had to look beyond the frame of a child orphaned by hateful need? What about the woman, the mother, who couldn't have been more than a child herself when she conceived? What about her? What of all the women breeding misery in childbed, force-fed that burdened, slippery plate of after-birth of which their husbands had washed their hands? And what right had she, that woman with her three fine daughters, her adoring husband, a rich house and all her beauty; what right had she even to speak of the others—the damned, clutching their bags of money, broken-jawed with laughter as the snakes pulsed up their thighs to suck their breasts? Mrs. Anderson stared and stared at the tympanum, finding only that small equation in the whole, forcing her eyes at last to the Christ cradling within the mandorla. His nose was broken, the lips slightly parted, almost wet, and the eyes abstracted in some dream. It was a Greek head, out of all time and trouble. She turned away and walked down the cathedral stairs. She did not want that Christ, those carvings—she would not stomach them.

In front of her was the square, made of stones that had surely known far more water than sun. Yet there was a fresh-ness, a careless imprint to everything that resisted the small, fine rain: a man in a bright-blue workman's suit, hot blue, sweeping the cobbles with a flattened broom; children chasing each other around the fountain; the smell of bread from out the windows of every bakery in town. And the short, sudden clamour of bells, telling the hour. She put her hand to her mouth, as if to prevent some cry, some stupid grief at the separateness and fear and blank refusal she felt shaking her, loosening her very edges. It seemed to her years before she could board that train to Vézelay.

There was a circular, walled walk around the cathedral and out onto the square. Mrs. Anderson pulled up the collar of her coat and started round. They had asked her only about the nominal parts of herself, the night before—she had told no lies. She was married; had two children, boys, studying at university. Now she was doing what she had always promised herself to do—studying, looking, travelling. But with no-one's blessing, save that of the anonymous trustees of a memorial fund.

43

Her husband was a Lutheran minister, in Winnipeg. One Monday she had tidied and then walked out of his house, which had never been hers. Her children did not accept or understand what she had done, although they must have known she had long ceased to love them with that fierce possessiveness in which mothers consume the dumb, helpless creatures given to their care. Once they had started school they had been no longer her own; somehow there had never been any other love with which to fill her emptied breasts. Her own fault; her husband's, too. She had admired, respected and—married him. He had let her know, once the children were born, that her respect and admiration were now quite beside the point. She had become the mother of his children, a third party to his life. She had lost her religion almost as an afterthought, but her twenty years in that house she had eaten as bitter herbs to her daily bread. A woman did not leave her husband for such unsubstantial reasons when she would compromise his livelihood by doing so: a mother did not rip her children from their father, especially when that mother did not, with any hunger, want those children. Nor did she sell them—nor did she squat over a trashcan to be rid of them.

Not that she'd attempted anything so theatrical, scheming her freedom. There had only been the black, bitter gladness at miscarrying the last child, the one her husband had never known of, the child conceived obtusely, dutifully in that last spurt of semen, that last burdening of womb before what her husband called "the vessels of creation" were at last rinsed and stacked and neatly put away forever. She had waited out those twenty years and then, summoning circumstances and the ghost of a desire, put together the few things that were her own, and walked away. To the university, of all sanctuaries. She had been lucky—obtained loans and grants, and now awards. She had trumpeted nothing, accused no-one, refusing commiseration as she did all confidences. She had been wrong to marry; in her time it had been better for certain women to dry slowly up, hidden, quiet, like a nut within a shell, than marry. Women, young women, were lucky now but they had better look to it that their luck should last. As long as you had a womb someone would be after you to fill it with something—babies, blood or yeasty mother-love for all the wretched and abandoned of the earth. Mater Misericordia with her skirts spread sexlessly over them all. Gothic Eve, big-bellied with fruit and pit of the sin they'd forced into her mouth. Far better those carvings of the Romanesque she'd chosen for her field of study. In bodies squat, shaved of all beauty or else rayed long, large, empty like Christ's eyes above the doors of Autun cathedral, she could look for tangible reflections of another kind of woman, someone no-one had yet seen or taken.

The rain that had been dripping listlessly all morning had by now taken form: you could hear it tap upon the stone, finding fissures to widen and ornaments to gouge away. Mrs. Anderson tied her scarf a little tighter under her chin. So here she was, again: cold, wet, alone, in need of temporary shelter. It would have to be the Musée Rolin, just across the square. Today was Sunday, there would be no entrance fee—she could use the money on another cup of hot and bitter coffee after her visit. For the third time that week she walked inside the tall wrought-iron gates to see what she'd already tired of: Gothic madonnas upstairs, some fine late-medieval Burgundian carving and the Eve, of course. She'd studied so many reproductions of that carving that her actual encounters with it had been elbowed-out by expectation. She thought she might try again, one last time. A guard came with her into the room, to switch on the electric light for her. She thanked him in her bad French, wondering whether the man would at least have smiled in return had she been younger, or attractive—a woman like Bridie. The guard shuffled out and Evelyn turned to the wall where she knew she would find the Eve.

Rounding a lump of stone that had been salvaged from

some enormous, ruptured design: neither lying, nor floating free, but attached to earth by one bent elbow and her pliant knees. Her body long, small, strong. A line running down from her throat, between the sure spheres of her breasts, sketched a rib cage, underlined the sturdy, snaking, cone-filled tree sprung from the base of the stone block. Under that tree her hips turned so that while her arms and trunk were full-face, toward you, her legs came down in profile: slender thighs descending from the shadows of leaves. Calves strong and well-shaped, rising from bent knees and disappearing off the sculpted block as if abducted by that serpent mounting her broken ankles up into the tree. Her head in three-quarters view: eyes huge, globed, looking to some focal point the viewer could not find, unless she lay herself down like this Eve in some small, free space above the ground, and dreamed. Next her hair: supple, close to the head, then rivering across one shoulder. Undulant, slow fire, unlike the end-stopped wave of snake into tree. Her small mouth closed, as if she had no need to speak or make sound; her left hand, drawn up along her face—not pillow-ing or cradling, but as if helping her to see. And framing her, the short and corded curves of trees, swaying, swaying so that she seemed to rock between them, slowly, with such control that the snake itself seemed only to ape her move-ments. In one implicit gesture she plucked the apple, her arm reaching back to the strange, conical fruit that the very rhythm of branch and trunk propelled into her large hand. Her arms reaching back as her eyes dreamed forward; her movements, mirrors: movements you watch yourself make, doors you observe on one side as you pass through them from the other. And all this within some perfect rhythm, beyond judgement or correction: the act of plucking, the act of dreaming—one hand reaching back to the tree, one for-ward, gesturing to some point beyond this fashioning or any other.

Evelyn stepped forward, stretching out her fingers to

touch the body of this Eve—to feel the cool, grained flesh within her hands, to touch those perfect moons of eyes and take the impress of their vision. Within minutes the guard came back into the room to hurry her along; it made him nervous to have people spend time with the things he was paid to watch. He coughed, then rattled off a list of other masterpieces to be found in the museum: the famous Madonna, the Nativity of the Maître de Moulins, the....

She thanked him, but she didn't want anything else just now. She left the room and the museum and walked back out to the square, looking up into the street, away from the cathedral. On the sidewalk, laughing, their arms full of parcels, were two women: one of them looked like Bridie. Evelyn scrambled round a corner and found a taxi parked in a cul-de-sac. The driver finished rolling his cigarette, scratched his head and agreed to take her to the station.

She shut her eyes tight as the cab jerked up the road, and let the moment's images print themselves under her eyelids. Bridie, of course: warm, rich, beautiful. One of the lucky ones of a snuffed generation, created not from the grudging, crowded ribs of man, but out his scheming head. He gave you the capacity for love in proportion as you were lovable; you were lovable in the degree you filled some plaster cast of sacrifice: lover, wife, mother, wise-woman—layered like an onion, with a transparency where pith should be. What was it they said about good women—how they soared, exploded and then fizzled into air like spent rockets, once they'd birthed and reared their children; homed their husbands. What of the others—those women to whom it was given not just to bleed children out, but to batter them forever after? Mater Misericordia. Damn Bridie and the domestic halo brightening her face. What had she ever known of that maimed laughter, that black gladness of being free of what you could never want, never be?

And think instead, before the taxi stopped, of that imagining of woman with no womb to fill or wounds to make;

filling the space between earth and the low branches of thick-fruited trees.

Other fruit, other earth: the fashioning of unseen dreams.

Viper's Bugloss

The first thing he remembered to see was the jack pine in stiff shock against the fence: it was still there, still there, a pledge that everything else would be waiting for him, just as it once had been. "Look, Sally—Jerome, do you see? That goddamned beautiful bald tree—it hasn't changed at all!" They didn't see, and besides, Sally didn't feel like putting herself out for one jack pine among the hundred she'd already seen on the drive up: she was conjecturing the size of the cabin, judging that Nick had exaggerated its spaciousness just to lure her up into the bush for a week. It had been hard enough to take time off from the offices—his and hers —and Jerome would be missing the first week of the summer school they'd decided to invest in for him—the kid needed some stimulation: as Nick kept on complaining, he had no imagination. A week up here, without Pac-Man or video cassettes, just the wash of the lake and the stretch of the sand. She had had her doubts. Turning around to look at him she found the child obstinate as ever, stretched out on the back seat and staring up at the upholstery of the car roof, not even caring to pretend to be asleep.

Five minutes later they were out of the car, their arms full of suitcases, beach towels, books and groceries and inflatable rafts. It was only a dash from the car to the porch, but Nick's keys wouldn't open the front door and by the time they'd discovered the back one, the mosquitoes had had their feast. Then, going up the concrete steps, Jerome managed to drop the one bottle of Off!; as Nick bent down to clear up the glass he identified the weeds sprouting all along the path they'd just negotiated as poison ivy.

"Hot water and soap, hot water and soap and we'll be just fine," he kept singing into Sally's ears: she was ready to wash out his mouth with the stuff, except that of all the things to have left behind, they'd forgotten the soap. Still, some ten minutes later Nick had a kettle steaming and was lathering their shins with some detergent he'd discovered below the sink. Then they dumped their gear in the bedrooms, turned on whatever lights were working and, shivering into bathing-suits, picked their way down the steep slope of sand to the lake.

He knew better than to exult: he let that water and this sky sing out for him. Jerome had run headlong into the lake and was swimming strongly out: not bad for a ten year old, thought Nick, trying to remember what distance he'd been able to make at that age. With his brother and sister he'd raced between the Fairlie cottage and Elephant Rock, a good half mile; using a steady crawl stroke, too, none of this changing-over every couple of yards. He watched the wake his son had left behind: just a slight snag on the water. You couldn't believe the stillness and completeness: even the air seemed to have its arms full of everything there was in the world to be caught and held onto. A moment or an hour later there was the sound of water being poured from a glass pitcher: Sally, entering the lake at last. Her bathing-suit was black: it made him think of a mourner's armband on a white shirt-sleeve. Too thin and too pale; she worked too hard although there was no need, now that his business was taking off at last. But that was the way she wanted it—and he had hardly known her any heavier: even when eight months pregnant with Jerome, she'd been addressed as "Miss" in stores—or so she had boasted. And Jerome, now, swimming free of them both: you would never believe that they had made him out of one careless embrace. Feeling comfortably sentimental, Nick settled down on a driftwood log and let his memory out with his stomach: twenty, twenty-two years since he'd last seen this place. When his mother had died the three children had decided to sell the cabin, the half-acreage of forest and the strip of beach that had made up the property. His older brother had handled the sale—badly, as it turned out, for the buyer had got rid of the place at three times the price they'd asked, just five years later.

The Fairlie place was still standing, though who could tell if it had remained in the family: perhaps tomorrow he'd walk over there. If any of them were still there—what was the daughter's name, she'd been about his age—they would surely remember him. They could get together, have a drink; it would be pleasant to have someone to talk to. Annie—her name had been Annie. Still is, he corrected himself: daft to assume she'd dropped out of existence just because he'd forgotten her. Daft was one of her words, Annie's—the family had emigrated from some place in the north of Scotland, he remembered: there had been nine of them altogether. And his family had been five: why was it that people had so few children, nowadays, or none at all?

Sally was waving to him from the sandbar: her voice tumbled gently into the still air, giving a tenderness to tired words: "Come on in, it's as warm as soup!" Still bobbing among memories, he recalled the packages of instant soup-mix he'd carried in from the car. His mother had simmered beef bones for them—they would have the marrow scraped over toast for a snack before supper, and listen to "Calling All Britons" over the radio: his mother had been a war bride, and had left her whole family behind her to come to Canada. She and Mrs. Fairlie would drink tea together in the afternoons while the kids played together on the sandhills, or explored the shoreline around Gulbransen's General Provisions, chewing on ropes of red licorice that you could buy for a penny. Gulbransen's was gone—the old man had died the same year his own father had, the last year they'd all been up at the cabin together. Still, there could be no harm in walking along the shore to where the shop had been—with Jerome. The kid was much too far out; Sally should have followed him: he stood up and cupped his hands and called out the boy's name, but though he was sure he'd been heard, Jerome kept on swimming away. There was nothing for it but to get into the water and bring him back, though he felt a peevish reluctance to get wet: it was too comfortable just sitting on that log, remembering things, alone. After all, the others couldn't feel the way he did—it was just a cabin by a lake to them, and he couldn't blame anyone for that but himself. They'd been fools to sell the place and lose all this.

The water was only slightly cooler than Sally had promised: it was like being extinguished, sliding in, or like turning transparent as an empty glass—no name or business or relation anymore, just a substance to be buoyed up. Then he began to swim, exuberantly: he'd always been a strong swimmer, with never a moment's fear of the water. His father had taught them all to swim before they could properly walk; the first thing he'd always do, coming up to join them here on weekends, would be to strip off his workclothes, race down to the water and swim a mile or more, even in the roughest waves. The poor bastard had never had more than a week at a stretch up here; if he'd taken longer holidays they'd never have had the money to keep the place on. And then, the first winter of his retirement, shovelling the walk one night, he'd slipped on a handspan of ice and burst one small blood vessel in his brain. He'd died still unconscious, two days later, in hospital.

Nick reached Jerome and gave him a tow back to the sandbar, the way you'd rescue an exhausted swimmer. He felt the child's arms on his shoulders and the strangeness of this: when was the last time he'd ever touched him? Again, he thought of his father, and the way the children had all ridden on his shoulders in the water. He swam faster, until it became too shallow: as the both of them stood up he reached for Jerome's hand to walk with him over the stones into shore, but the boy didn't know to wait, just hobbled in on his own. Sally was there with enormous towels for them: they rubbed themselves as dry as they could and started up the hill. "Listen—" Nick made them stop halfway up. You could hear water lap at each stone; somewhere in the distance a motorboat droned and a sandpiper gave odd little cries, to which it seemed to expect no response. The sand slid every which way under their feet, they had to push down hard to keep from slipping, helping one another till they reached the fence behind which the coarse grass began. Nick was the last one inside: standing on the porch, the doorhandle in his fingers, he stopped a moment and looked out between the jack pine's seedy boughs to the lake. "It's good to be here: good to be back," he spoke out loud. But he couldn't hang onto the words, they sank into the calm of the evening like a rounded stone into the sandy bottom of a pool. The only noise on the air came from the door as it snapped on its hinges, shut.

It couldn't have worked out otherwise: he had the luck to wake first that morning and, as Sally was huddled up against the wall with all the covers, he could slip into the bathroom with his clothes without waking her. In the narrow corridor he paused outside Jerome's room: the cedar walls didn't quite reach up to the ceiling, you could hear the merest toss or turn from one room to the next. The child was breathing softly, regularly, no doubt exhausted from the long drive and the evening's swim. Once in the bathroom Nick stumbled over a tin bucket that had been placed just inside the door: he started to curse, but ended by laughing, sitting on the edge of the window sill to rub his toe. So that leak in the ceiling was still there, the one his father had never got round to repairing. He looked up critically; if there were tools around perhaps he would fix it—not for the present owner's ease, but as something owed to his own father.

It was the cabin's only view of the lake, this short oblong cut into the bathroom wall: whoever first modernized the place ought to have designed it the other way around, with the parlour where the toilet was. His mother would pull a face, shrug shoulders: why else had they got it so cheap? They'd bought it from the nephew of two ancient spinsters —the Misses Spencer, he remembered—who'd practically been born in the cabin, and who'd told of having once spent a winter up here. A spew of blackish drops in the basin: this time he did curse: he'd cut his chin with the razor, wasn't used to one but had been damned if he was going to bring an electric shaver to this place. He peered into the shard of mirror tacked over the sink: deep enough, he'd have to put a bandage on. Sally would see and laugh at him, having told him this would happen while they were packing to come. But he had nothing to staunch the blood, the cut stung, he felt betrayed as well as wounded—until he discovered, tucked into the pocket of his shaving kit, a wad of bandaids: Sally, having the last laugh after all. He dabbed the blood, pressed on the bandage and managing to avoid more bloodshed as he finished shaving, even began to whistle under his breath. Think of it, good Christ: two thin-blooded spinsters—in their sixties—spending a god-damned winter up here: no insulation (you could see light splintering between mortar and logs) and an outdoor privy smack in the poison ivy. What had they done with them-selves all winter long besides shake and shiver and cajole a fire from the hearth? People had been different then, made of better stuff—think of his own parents, no hell of a life for them: never enough money, three kids to dress and feed and send to school, no holidays away from the kids (he and Sally usually spent their summer vacation at a lodge with Jerome, the kind of place where the kids have a separate playground and dining-room and all the bedrooms are soundproofed). Whatever had his own folks done, his father coming up from the hot, dank city, spending his two nights a week with his woman in a bed whose springs would sing out for miles around if they so much as rubbed shoulders? He thought of Sally, shivering in the satin baby-doll pyjamas she'd insisted on bringing, wrenching the covers away from him in the night: he felt a shallow stab of guilt—it wasn't a real holi-day up here, having to cook for themselves and leave the place in reasonable order; there'd be no dancing after dinner, no tennis courts, no sailboats or sundecks. But, then, at least it was a change—better still it was something real, the three of them together here with only each other for com-pany and help. Why, he'd take Jerome into the woods that very afternoon, show him the place where you could find raspberries growing—

Shaved, washed, dressed, he strode into the kitchen, put the kettle on and looked over the shelves while the water came to a boil. Sally had arranged their own provisions on an empty shelf, but the other ledges were full of unfamiliar plates and cups, most of them chipped and cracked, none of a pattern: the usual cottage ware. He recognized a certain sparse and deliberate order in these shelves, painted a dead-white; narrow, bearing ancient and unused jars of split peas or pearl barley. They seemed all necessary and good: they had reason to be there, unlike most of the things on the tables and in the cabinets of their apartment in the city: expensive, time-saving electrical appliances; computerized games and gadgets; crystal and glass from the January sales; everything braying its cost and their success in meeting it. The kettle sent up clouds to divert him; into a coronation mug he spooned instant coffee and milk, then came the silver spurt from the kettle. Simple acts, simple objects— he felt absurdly happy.

He sat down with his second cup of coffee on an uncom-fortable, overpadded sofa in the parlour: it had always been the darkest room in the place, with its low, slitted windows screened by leaves and twigs. This furniture was all unfamiliar—they might have left the old stuff there, it had all been part of the sale. He felt an unreasonable grudge against the owner, a man he knew only from an ad in the paper: "Charming heritage log-cabin for rent by week or month; a holiday the whole family won't forget: moderate terms." On a hunch Nick had dialed the number, heard a closer description and hadn't been able to resist a return to the old place, despite Sally's level suspiciousness and Jerome's indifference. Of course he'd had his qualms as they drove up and found, for miles around, the ordered suburban lots run up by the developers: blank, glossy names like "Georgian Sands," "Hemlock Court," "Lakeside Manor"— the joke of it, driving for hours along a super highway only to find the same sweet home at the journey's end. But their own road was the same, the forest still virgin, so that they would be wakened by birds and not someone else's television every morning. It must have been by some negligent Provi-dence that things here were so unchanged; if the place hadn't prospered much, neither had it suffered. Perhaps it was the ghost of his family life that had protected it, the influence of people whose relations with each other were direct and simple, day to day: husband and wife, parents and children. He looked for confirmation to the little niche hollowed out in the great stone chimney over the fireplace. It couldn't be—he never would have bet on it, but there it was, still sheltering inside, the little china figure his mother had won at a raffle—a cross between Charlie Chan and the Buddha. His mother had believed it brought them good luck, and perhaps it had. For, looking at all things equally, who could have had a happier childhood? His parents had given him not only food and clothes and toys but this as well: a steady structure under his feet and all around—to every act, a genuine response, whether enlightened or not it scarcely seemed to matter, now. That things had fallen apart after their deaths was no-one's fault. His sister had moved out west, married a lawyer: she sent him a Christmas card every other year, with snapshots of her kids. He and his brother lived in the same city but only met for stilted family meals at New Year's and Easter: their wives didn't get along at all and Jerome was much younger than his cousins. Damn it, he'd phone his brother soon as he got back; he'd tell him about the cabin, persuade him to help buy it back—it had been the mistake of their lives ever to have lost this place. Sally would surely agree once she'd been here for a bit. He could hear her now, stumbling along the corridor, pouring coffee in the kitchen, cursing because there was no artificial sugar. What did it matter—she was his wife, no stranger: she would make allowances, and understand.

It had been a halcyon morning—he liked to use that phrase, it said so exactly what he felt and dignified it in the process. They'd gone down to the beach, swum, lain in the sun: he'd even coaxed Jerome to help build a fortress in the sand. At lunch the soup had been lumpy and the cheese dry, but he at least hadn't cared. He'd announced to Sally at the very end that he and Jerome would be going berry-picking, thinking the child would enjoy the surprise, the sudden conspiracy, and not having dared to risk an outright refusal by asking Jerome beforehand. What could he say now—of course he would go, silent or not. Sally had given them plastic containers with a wry face, as if to ask what the sudden father-son business was all about, but he had just smiled at her, cursing her inwardly for a suspicious bitch. Lovely Sally, slim as any of these saplings and about as sturdy: she hadn't wanted to breast-feed Jerome and didn't want another child, and that was that. Up till now he hadn't had any ammunition against her constant gibes: "What, you really want another? You hardly know what the one we've already got looks like, and you still want to play at being a father?" Well, he was refuting that now as he led the child, all unwilling, through the thicket to where the path began.

What was the matter with the boy, was he afraid of poison ivy—of him? No doubt he'd rather be back in the city, reading a comic book in front of the television. "Come on, don't drag your feet, you're turning this into a funeral." Weeds and brambles had gorged on the path—they had to fight their way along, and Nick himself got forearms and hands scratched while his eyes furred with mosquitoes and his ears thickened with their whine. If there were any berries, they had been eaten up long before. An enormous, rotting stump was now blocking their way: one second too late he recognized the drone of wasps rising within—and Jerome allergic to their sting. "Run, run!" he shouted, nearly kicking the boy ahead of him: if he got badly stung they would have to drive back right away and see a doctor. Sally should have reminded him, what sort of a mother was she to let her kid go off like this into the bush? They ran and ran, tripping over sapped branches and clumped stones but managing somehow to get back onto the main road, panting and sweating and ridiculous, with the little cartons all cracked now by their flight. Jerome seemed to have been crying and Nick, feeling responsible, wheeled furiously around, searching for something to justify the scare, to put a brighter face on things so that they could face Sally with some slight show of success. At the turn-off to the cabin he stopped willfully and stabbed with his hands into the undergrowth. By sheer luck he found something there. "Look, Jerome, what's this, what do you see?" The boy stared up into his father's eyes: twisting his mouth half into a pout, half into an accusation, he said nothing. And then, grabbing Jerome's T-shirt: "What the hell do you see—look, goddamn you, haven't you got eyes?" The child looked sullenly down into the clump of grass; stringing his father's patience, he at last mumbled out the one word: "Weeds."

Nick loosened his grip, let his hands hang at his sides. "Weeds? What kind of smart-ass answer is that? Is that what they teach you in science class? Why, when I was your age I knew the names of a hundred wildflowers—maybe more, Jesus Christ, kid. Why, my father and brother and sister and I would go out every Sunday morning here and just walk along the side of this road looking for them—Queen Anne's lace, chickory, buttercups. Look, it's Christ-bitten buttercup, didn't you even know that?" He stooped, ripped up the plant and thrust it into his son's face—and then relaxed his hand so that the flower fell brightly into the dust. He brought his hand slowly, unsurely, to the boy's head; he stroked the hair softly until he could no longer ignore the scowl on Jerome's face, then dropped his hand and stood stupidly at the roadside, admitting his fault, his utter failure, in the steady misery of the child's face before him. He felt like weeping, like howling—"Why my father and brother and sister and I...." And then Jerome touched his arm, quickly, and pointed over to a spar of brilliant blue. "What's that one called?" he challenged. His father, glad of the chance to change his face, walked over to where his son was pointing; parted the stems of grass and tilted the strange plant toward him. On an ugly, haired stalk a cup of violet and magenta and impossibly bright blue blared out. Its scent was strong, unpleasant even, but the flower was so curiously shaped, so outrageously coloured that it drew his eyes away from everything else. "What is it?" Jerome repeated, uneasily. "I can't remember," Nick at last replied, and then, sitting back on his haunches, he whistled. "Bugger if it isn't viper's bugloss. Viper's bugloss—I haven't seen this since I was your age—younger." "No, don't pick it!" Jerome wailed as he watched his father twist at the stem. "It might be poisonous—it looks poisonous, I don't like it!" "Nonsense," Nick overrode him, working the stem away from the earth at last, staining his hands with its acrid-smelling juice. "No, you're thinking of belladonna —that's the deadly one." He held the flower straight up into the sun, admiring the sheer bright violence of it. "Let's take this home to your mother," he finished: "we'll put it in a jam-jar on the parlour table—quick now, let's hurry."

But the child had been right—if not precisely poisonous, it was a bringer of no good omen. As they hurried down to the water for their evening swim, the air seemed thicker than it had the night before; you could feel raindrops clinging together. They stayed too long in the water and came out chilled, Sally in a foul temper, having grazed her ankle on a rock. And as the clean sand sifted under their feet, making them lunge and strain to get up the hill, they heard the weird undulant cries of loons on the water, suddenly terrifying as the glint of a knife in a late-night subway car back in the city.

In the middle of that night it began to rain—Nick and Sally woke together, and Sally rolled over, groaning—"I knew this would happen—you just wait and see, it'll rain all week and then where will our holiday be?" He didn't answer her immediately, but ten minutes later reached for her and caught only a glide of satin as she shook off his hands. She was too tired, she said: she couldn't sleep on this rusty, lumpy excuse for a bed, anyway. She just didn't want to, she insisted, as Nick began to pull her toward him: and besides, the soap wasn't the only thing they'd managed to forget. Her pills were on the dresser back in the apartment. He let it go at that, but wouldn't let her settle back into sleep: "Would it be such a catastrophe if you conceived a child?" he spoke out to the rain.

"What?" She sat up in the slanting bed, clutching the sheet to her, looking to Nick like a prudish corpse. "Are you crazy? Don't you realize that Jerome can hear every word we're saying?"

"So, what's so shameful about having a family—it'd do the kid good to have a brother—sister."

"You're mad, Nick, just sheer, stupid, God—-I don't know what! With a ten-year gap? I don't believe it. As if you'd be willing to give up your work and mind a baby. Well, would you, would you? You're not fair, you never have been. If you dare—oh, let's go back to sleep, you must be having a nightmare and talking in your dreams—go to bed, goodnight: let's not wake Jerome."

He listened to her fake an even breathing and then, annoyed at paying even this attention, turned away from her and pretended, himself, to sleep. An hour later he groped his way to the kitchen, poured himself a scotch—that they hadn't managed to forget—and then went into the parlour. The Buddha was still up there, gleaming blankly in the dark. He rubbed his hands over his face and sat for a long while. When at last he uncovered his eyes the first thing he saw was the viper's bugloss in its jar on the dinner table. He walked over to it, plucked it up from the water and twirled the hairy stem between his fingers. The flowers had shut fast, tight, in the blackness. "No," he said, "you're not poisonous; it's just us, Sally and me: whatever's between us —or whatever's not." All the same he couldn't sleep till he'd taken the flower, jar and all, and thrown the whole thing into the bush outside the kitchen door. The rain was still falling, making a noise like steel pins showering a glass floor. He locked the door, shut off the light in the kitchen and went to sleep on the green, over-upholstered sofa in the parlour.

In the morning it was worse: endless rain. They had brought books to read—Nick had been grandiose and taken only Shakespeare and the Bible: Sally settled down with Agatha Christie. The light in the parlour was bad; with this rain the dramatic gloom that sank the room on the sunniest of days turned merely dreary, dirtying everything—the maps on the wall, the farmer's daughter calendar-photos, the old-English prints of "Nature's Bounty" that Nick's mother had hung on the walls—cottages profuse with clematis and wisteria, with sentimental lovers in eighteenth-century costume, sighing together at a wishing-well. After 40 minutes Nick slammed *The Tempest* shut and began to rummage among the old, old *Life* magazines and yellowed *Maclean's* inside the buffet. After an hour he developed a headache: Jerome was stomping around, bored to death, and Sally had decided to do her nails, so that the reek of varnish drove little steel-heads of pain into his skull. The next morning they were on the road. Whenever Sally switched on the radio, the report was the same: showers through the week, clearing slightly Saturday: the high 68, the low—

Well, he'd had it, royally. It was the same jack pine beside the fence, the same cabin, even the same water: he wouldn't argue that. It was there, a rock for him to stand on, to survey the general, confused ruin of his adult life. His parents' deaths; selling the cottage and loosing the last ties with the family; marrying Sally, pretty, clever Sally; having Jerome and losing Jerome between all their business trips and overtime and weekend assignments.... All for the good life, soft and shiny: summers at a lodge and winters in Mexico with Jerome thrown to the mercy of housekeepers and what some ironist in PR had called the "home" computer. Clear as the weather report; he'd made his choices. But why, how? He could have stayed at the cottage, always; married Annie Fairlie; raised five kids and taught them all the names of wildflowers—

Daft. Idiot. Kill himself with work, as his father had, and all for nothing? Have his wife turn miserable and blowsy, raising children, simmering soup bones? How real could his own childhood have been, what fictions were his memories, for him to have thrown over every trace of them when it had come his turn to leave, marry, raise a child? Family love—strong and durable as some cooking-pot or kettle; or the coupled loneliness of his own marriage—which was the real, the only possibility? The car swerved over a greasy bit of road—it would be easy to have an accident in this rain, thinking such confusing things. He turned up the radio and shut off everything except the road and the shifting gears of Muzak.

Late that night, back in the neutral, calm décor of his apartment, his marriage, his life, he couldn't sleep. The same rain that had doused his holiday was rattling down the apartment windows. He lit the bedside lamp, saw the case of Sally's pills that she had remembered to take, this time. He turned his head to where she lay, crouched up against his body's heat, her face curiously soft and full. She had been right, of course: you didn't start things you knew you couldn't carry out. He eased himself as cautiously as he could out of their bed and covered her, as charitably as he would a stranger, with the blankets. He thought he should go check on Jerome, but was terrified of finding him awake, so went instead to what they called his study—a large closet, really, in which were crammed the virgin upright piano, a reproduction antique desk on which an unframed photograph of Sally and Jerome curled helplessly, and the few books he'd not sold or given away on leaving university. He put back the Shakespeare he'd taken so extravagantly to the cottage, and pulled out *The Native Wildflowers of Central Canada*—a book, the flyleaf told him, which he'd won as a graduation prize on leaving high school, centuries ago.

Dithering through the index, he found at last the entry that he wanted:

> Viper's Bugloss (Echium vulgàre) Borage or Forget-Me-Not Family (Boraginàceae) A tall, erect, very rough, bristly, leafy plant, simple or branched. The lance-shaped, bristly pointed leaves are up to 4½″ long, progressively smaller and sessile upward. Strikingly showy, purplish blue flowers are bell- shaped. June to September.

This was it, exactly. He found comfort in the finality bred by such precise detail, the Latin terms, the absence of alternative or choice. These things were as they were, could be no different; to question would be to undo them, entirely. He put his finger to the text and read aloud: "Habitat: Dry fields, waste places." But this wasn't right—wasn't fair: it read like a judgment, or a warning. He shut his eyes, trying to remember the feel, the look of that flower he'd tugged up: rough-haired, grotesquely brilliant, utterly unexpected, like a signal flare, a siren in his eyes. A book fell off the shelf behind him and he jumped as if a gun had gone off in his ears.

Not a book; or rather, a book knocked over by the boy, Jerome, standing there in his pyjama bottoms, his white skin looking so delicate it seemed as if the glare from the electric light would bruise it. He stood before Nick's chair, expectant, frozen, like a small animal in the headlights of an oncoming car.

"Jerome," began Nick, afraid to touch and startle him.

"I can't sleep."

"No. Me too. Jerome—" Words of one syllable; his name—begin at the beginning, not like the last time. But what now, with the child standing here in front of him, staring, wanting, silent—

"Look; come over here. Close enough so you can see this

picture. Remember that weed—that flower we found in the woods? Maybe you've forgotten—"

"Viper's bugloss." Jerome lifted his long, awkward arms and folded them across his chest, as if to hug his pleasure in having remembered the name. And Nick, carefully as if he were transplanting some fragile plant, dangling its roots in a shock of rough, cold air, reached up and patted his son's shoulder.

"Smart kid. That's the way. Why, when I was your.... Look, Jerome, I know what we'll do. Tomorrow we'll go down the ravine out back—forget the summer school, it's not important—to the ravine, and find as many kinds of different wildflowers as we can—we'll take this book. If it rains? We'll go to the museum—they've got rooms and rooms of plants there—everything. Okay?"

Jerome shrugged; Nick kept his hand on the boy's shoulder. "Okay?"

"Sure, I guess. If you want. Okay."

Nick gently withdrew his hand from Jerome's shoulder, closed the book and pulled himself out of his chair.

"Now let's turn out the lights and go to bed. Lunatic, being up this late—it's past two o'clock. You can tuck yourself in? Of course you can, of course. Goodnight, then — don't wake your mother—don't forget, tomorrow morning—"

As Nick slid back into bed and stretched out toward sleep he thought, one last time, of the cabin. It didn't belong to him, anymore—it never really had. It was here, in the city, this apartment, that he had to stake out something, to make a start—with Jerome; with Sally, reaching out for him in sleep now, as she could never do, once woken. Here, now —he had to begin. His eyes closed over images, precise, detailed, as if he were dying, seeing for the last time the still, blank lake, the Buddha over the fireplace, the bald jack pine against the cabin fence. All in the lightning glare of that intractable, bruise-coloured flower.

Somewhere in Italy

There is a photograph in some drawer or other, taken during their holiday—that day they had the argument. She's standing on the balcony of their *pensione,* spreading cheese and bread and apricots over the tablecloth, and not wanting to be photographed. But she poses for him all the same, so that her shoulders and her head do not cut off the view. Around her the small hills with their precisely planted trees assume the soft brightness of gold: the picture must have been taken just before sunset, when the light is roundest and fullest. There are marks that might be a distant *campanile* but which, perhaps, are only flaws in the film. Her face is in shadow—he took the photograph against the light—so that you cannot tell what her expression is: settled contentment, edgy sorrow or only that intimate absorption with immediate objects—tablecloth, breadknife, cheese—in which the old Dutch painters would eclipse their models. As for where the photograph was taken, neither of them can remember—they only know that it was somewhere in Italy.

Two years after their marriage they had saved up time and money for a month in Italy: a sentimental journey, if not a honeymoon. They chose Italy because neither of them had ever travelled there or knew very much about it: it would be something strange and new that they could learn together. At the very moment that the midnight train from Paris jolted them awake, cracking a bar of sun across their faces, they opened their book. Still half-asleep, they cranked up the blinds to stare across the rails into a woman's face, framed by green shutters and a pot of geraniums so red they seemed to sear the morning air. Sleep-swollen still, the face hung like a waterdrop as they rode slowly past, then blurred and fell out of their eyes.

They stayed in Venice for a week, choosing a hotel with the same pots of geraniums, the same green shutters. For that one week they made-believe themselves into Italians: walking back streets, devouring fresh pineapple and freezing melon in the parks, riding the Vaporetto to Torcello, wandering round St. Mark's Square too early in the morning for even German tourists to be up, and following the vendors wheeling fruit and vegetables to market in unpainted wooden carts. They told each other without need of words that they could never, never be happier. Time and place were ripening like the soft, small cheeses sold in baskets at the market stalls; they floated on their happiness just as the small, miraculously tethered islands of which Venice is composed are buoyed up on their hidden pilings. Small wonder that they fell in love, as all the picture postcards promised they would, with pink palazzos and damp basilicas, with frenzied city squares and the few, small gardens thrusting fingers of laurel and of oleander through barred gates. So much in love that when the fine weather broke they left at once, refusing to unlearn that circumambience of marbled light and water that was now their Venice.

Only after their departure, on a dilatory zigzag down from Florence to Urbino, taking speed-crazed buses over mountain roads and cheap trains run on esoteric schedules, did they discover differences in their response to Italy. He could not tolerate the heat, the heavy, wet balloon of air squatting on everything around him; she thrived on it, walking for hours on a few *gelati* in the afternoon, and then strolling about after supper, doing the *passagio* with all the other Italians in the hot, small towns. Small wonder that, with midnight rambles and dawn excursions, with she insisting on this or that museum during the siesta hours, he swallowing salt tablets and threatening collapse in whatever shuttered coolness their *pensiones* could afford, they had the quarrel.

It was in Citta di Castello or perhaps even in Ferrara, for there was a castle or a ducal palace there—it had been the locus of their argument. His only fault had been in listening to her pleas of how insane it was—how wasteful, stupid, wrong—to sleep away their last few days in Italy. Instead of rolling over on the too-short bed into a bog of dreams he had got up, gulped down a few more salt tablets and stumped outside, foul-tempered, into even bitchier heat. The hotel awnings, the oleander, even the sidewalks seemed to be stooping under the burden of a sun inviolate, enamelled. They forgot their map, took the wrong road and ended up in an industrial suburb of the town. Here there were factories and tenements instead of galleries and castles; children, dusty-legged, their hair unwashed; starving cats feeding on scraps of pasta flung into the middle of the road. It frightened her, it was so familiar—this could be a slum in

Toronto, Halifax or Montreal. The frowns incised on the children's faces, the scabbed, bald patches on the cats had nothing at all to do with the plush and easy phrasebook words he'd memorized: "A room with a bath, *per piacere.* May we see the wine list? I would like to buy some film for my camera."

Perhaps it wasn't even that they'd had too much of one another's company—perhaps it was their having tripped and scraped their shins on something postcards hadn't promised, texts they hadn't been prepared to read, that made the fight as short and stoppered as it was. He'd finally dug his heels in the middle of some endless dreary street as she was insisting that the palazzo had to be around the corner and back six blocks the way they'd come. He rallied the good North American oath, consigning the palace, the country, their holiday to the same overworked and sweaty fate of fornication. She yelled that she was going back to the palazzo on her own—he could curl up with the cats right there and dream of fettucine for all she cared. He turned his back and stomped away, knowing she'd turn up dust-streaked and apologetic sooner or later. Before he fell asleep in the child-sized hotel bed he was picturing how she would come and find him lying there, how—exhausted, guilty to the absolute of tenderness—she'd walk out of her clothes the way a swimmer walks out of the waves; come to join him in the narrow bed, curving her nakedness in toward his own.

But he slept and woke alone, rushed into his clothes and tore down to the lobby to find her sitting in a small wooden chair, her eyes fixed on a plaster madonna niched over the concierge's desk, her feet precise upon the floor. She must have come up to the room, bathed, changed and slipped out again, for she looked cool and fresh as a spring wind sitting there. Too cool; too fresh; she didn't say a word to him as they left the *pensione* and walked into the street. Then she announced in a hard, bright voice that they had better do some marketing—they couldn't afford to go to a *trattoria* for supper, their hotel room was costing them too much. Her tone made it quite clear she'd taken sides against that room and anyone who'd spent his afternoon asleep in it. At once he was furious again, appalled at her smallness, her ridiculous unfairness; wondering why it had taken this long time, this distance, for the selfishness, the childishness in her to show itself. Instead of the belligerent good humour he'd intended, he kept silence, taking his arm from her shoulder, enlarging the distance between them as they walked along.

It would take them ages to find a shop that was still open —people didn't start moving till well after six o'clock, after the siesta. She was ravenous after being on her feet all afternoon; the palazzo had been closed and so she'd wandered in and out and all around the cold, dank cathedral on the other side of the town before her pride allowed her to return to the *pensione*. He'd walked off with all their money, so that she hadn't been able to take a bus or even buy a cold drink and a slice of melon all afternoon. He wasn't bothering to ask her what she'd done all that time he'd snored away in bed—a young woman, an attractive young woman, on her own in Italy.... How was he to know that only paper-thin alley cats had rubbed up against her legs? They could never make this up, she knew that, even though they might let go the sulking and the stiffness—play their holiday parts: love on a Visa card abroad. They never fought at home, which made it all the pettier that they should quarrel here. One month of travelling together in this foreign place in which all they had in common was each other, spoiled so stupidly: one half-hour's foul temper in a small, hot town their final destination.

She took a scant, sideways look at him as they walked along; this distance between them felt like a railing, with sharpened spikes to keep intruders out. And she knew as well as she knew Italy that it would be like this for the rest of their life together, that marriage could be nothing but a mapless wandering through mere suburbs of convenience. She felt her body stiffen and draw in—she knew she must appear not as a woman in the round, plumped and pillowed like a Titian Venus, but as one of those profile portraits, all beaked nose and humped forehead, desolately sharp and bright. She wanted to howl, to shake apart and smash the distance that was taking shape between them like a hand-blown, heavy bulb of glass.

They were walking, without caring, the same wrong way they'd gone that morning. At a dingy corner shop selling stale bread, hard cheese and sullen apricots people were lining up behind two separate counters. The couple took their place in the shorter line, their silence severing them still. Unable to look at one another, they eyed the other customers: housewives in carpet slippers, shrill children gesturing with sugar candy in their dirty hands, one small, middle-aged man with an amused, intelligent face. This man looked back at them with sharp, fine eyes that somehow seemed to slit the anger knotting them apart, to shrink and to enclose them like the lens of a camera. They stepped instinctively together to return his look—their bare arms touched, as sudden as a slap, but their eyes, fixed on the man's face, still locked one another out though pleading now for some key to turn and spring them—

Suddenly the man's eyes leapt, the pupils clicked in understanding. He nodded, and shook the string bag loose from his right hand. Like some street sparrow jumping from dust-puddles to a green-leaved branch, balancing one moment before flitting into open air, the man raised his hand to his lips, kissed and then flourished his fingertips. "Ch'e bella! Bella!" he saluted them. As if responding to some free, chance benediction, they joined hands while the woman at the counter asked for the third time how much of the provalone they wished to buy.

The man had vanished by the time they'd made their purchases. They left the shop with bread and cheese and apricots like plump, small suns; swinging hands, their fingers firmly linked. Nothing had happened, everything was changed. Even the light seemed to have softened, smudging the lines dividing things: the river and the castle, the statues and the air, even the stringy cats and the dust in which they padded. Several people whom they never noticed turned to look at them as they passed by: holiday lovers, their happiness seeming to splash over the rims of mouths and eyes, blurring their faces with a love as real, as imprecise, as some indulgently unfocused photograph.

Red River Cruise

Somebody screamed—but it was nothing, only the Weasel poking his head round the hallway door, warning that the bus was already waiting for them in the parking-lot. Lyuba began to squeal: she wasn't ready, she'd been told the wrong time, she wouldn't be able to put on her nail polish. "Don't worry, Lyuba," Annie had flounced at her, "you don't need nail polish to pick your nose—or have you something better to do with your fingers tonight?" The rest of the girls laughed, and Lyuba went all yellow in the face: the rest of the girls except Laura, who was Annie's best friend and yet who choked sometimes on the things Annie said—the way she said them. But they were, most of them, ready: with their stretch hairbands and dusky blushing-powder, teetery high-heels and sparkle-stockings and puff-ball dirndl skirts the girls went shrieking down the corridor, pushing and thumping through the door that the Weasel, in a ludicrous fit of gallantry, was holding open for them all. Sophie, the oldest and engaged, or as good as, to the evening's chaperone, cut him a swath of "Evening in Paris" as she swept down the stairwell, patting his head as she passed him by. He watched the rest of them follow after her and then closed the door, looking at his reflection in its glass. He was too hunched and small for any sports jacket to fit him, so he was wearing one of George's sweaters—the good woollen one that had shrunk in last week's wash. He ruffled the thin, slippery hairs on his head and tried to smoothe the knot at his neck that wasn't a tie, but his Adam's apple, throbbing as it always did to his excitement. For one long moment he smiled at the ghost of his reflection as if this were a magic mirror or the brilliant blacks of Sophie's eyes. And then the smile dropped and vanished, like a coin into a broken slot machine. Weasel opened the door, passed through and trailed the echo of the girls' high-heels down the stairs.

Summer-school was nearly over and, as the custom was, all the pupils of the college were to be treated to a moonlight cruise down the Red River—or at least as far down the river as was deemed necessary by the principal. He wasn't coming along; at the last moment he'd begged off with a severe migraine—really the runs, or so it was whispered—so that Boris and Stefan were given complete charge: directed to frisk the boys for bottles or bags, to make sure that none of the girls unbuttoned any further than the evening's heat decreed, to switch on all the lights half-way through the dance just to keep them on their toes, and to alternate in taking pocket flashlights along the decks, casing any suspect awnings, lifeboats, cabins. For it was not without its risks, this Red River cruise, as the principal well knew: no Flin Flon farmer or Toronto lawyer, no Minneapolis mechanic or Montreal entrepreneur would pay good money for a six weeks' drilling in the fundamentals of Ukrainian grammar, culture and religion so that his adolescent child could be goosed, caught goosing or worse on the cruise—and in the very last week of the course at that. They had managed in previous years by hiring a strolling accordion band to patrol the decks and flush out any suspect behaviour—had even caught one of the seminarians who acted as teachers and chaplains during their summer break, in a compromising clutch with one of the older girls, a floozie from Winnipeg, who knew her way by heart around the college since she'd taken the same course four summers running.

But that was all in the line of things. Boys would be boys, and girls bad—they had to have their parties, their games, their Saturday nights downtown; neither the college nor their parents could stop it. The thing to do, the principal had lectured, was to control it; to give the opportunity and then snatch it back. And so Boris and Stefan, in their dog collars and sports jackets and theological black serge trousers, were rounding up and settling down the students in pairs on the 40 seats of the old schoolbus that would deliver them to the water. Or at least Boris was, for Stefan was stuck standing limply by the driver, his eyes and ears fixed on the girl who had been first to enter the bus and take her seat on the row two up from the back. She was nodding at him, not with any smile or shyness, but with steady, grave anticipation; she had picked out those seats, dead-sure there no-one who mattered could see or overhear them. If things were to go the way she had cut out and stitched them during her night-wakings and day-plottings, they would have at least to clear their throats on the business before the cruise began.

The bus started to fill. Annie entered conspicuously, in her pink-and-purple dress, with her shoes dyed pink and purple to match. She was a doctor's daughter; her father had a large practice in Hamilton and lectured at the university—everyone knew he had a say on who got into medical school there, and who didn't. Annie was the Doctor's daughter. Laura followed at her elbow, dressed in nun-like, self-effacing white and navy; she drew herself in as she walked to the seat Annie had chosen in the middle of the bus, where they would be seen by and could watch everyone. And indeed, Annie began to whisper to Laura as they took their seats—Laura by the window, Annie on the aisle— "Will you take a look at that Olga! Doesn't she look like a preacher's wife already, with that lipless little mouth and those stainless-steel fingernails? Sophie says Olga's going to make Stefan propose to her on the cruise: poor guy, he's so far gone she'll make him think it was all his own idea, even as she's hooking the ring through his nose." Laura didn't want to and yet had to turn her head, pretending to look out the back window and fixing Olga's small, smooth, nut-coloured face, with its fierce little pinching look; seeing her very eyes, a blue fog around the pupil, and a clear black line scooping up the fog, cutting upon the white. Olga had her hair braided and wound around her head—her hair was the softest brown, a tawny colour, long and thick. Stefan had felt it against his cheek once when he had bent over her on the bus into town. Then she hadn't even looked up at the touch—and hadn't moved away, either; she had allowed him to meet her at the bus stop later on that afternoon so that they could have the ride back to the college together. Stefan couldn't stop looking at her, even though he was supposed to be keeping count of the numbers they had to return with that night—he had lost count after Olga had boarded. He couldn't even wait for Boris to take his place; he hurried down the aisle, too thin, too tall, slamming his shins and elbows, down to the back where Olga was sitting. She looked now as if she didn't even see him there, she was freezing his grin into the arms of the cross—but still, she didn't

76

push him away as he sat down beside her.

The driver honked the horn and the bus started up; they were on their way before Annie could finish what she was telling Laura—something about George; what an asshole he was; how she had let him have it when he'd tried to come up to her room after hours on Sunday night. She said she'd just spat at his invitation to be his date on the cruise—had invited him to take that cow-pat, Lyuba, instead—did she see the two of them, two seats ahead on the right? Did she know what the guys called Lyuba? George himself had told her before they'd broken up; he'd told how all the guys had sat around in the vestry one Saturday night before chapel, drinking beer and naming all the girls—did she want to know what they called her? "No!" cried Laura, fearing it was herself they had named, expecting the cruellest words, trusting that Annie's prettiness, her grating tongue, her pastel-leather shoes and $20-a-week spending money might shield her, poor Laura-best-friend-tag-along, from their savage attention. "The Grand Canyon!" Annie bellowed, so that Lyuba squirmed against George's shoulder and he had to fight to keep her from turning round and abusing Annie in kind. "And do you know why they call her that?" Laura nodded violently to prevent something worse than she was imagining, but Annie must have taken pity on her, for she only laughed, saying, "No you don't, little mouse; you good, little Laura—don't worry, I won't tell you anything you don't want to know." And she went on to describe what a miserable night it would be, how the river would stink and the wind cut through their thin dresses, how there'd be nothing to drink but that ratpiss red wine left over from the last party. She made Laura promise that the two of them would stick together so it wouldn't be a total loss—they could spend the time thinking of ways to get Laura's parents to let her spend two weeks at Annie's house before going back to Toronto. They would have a fantastic time; Annie would introduce her to this guy who was mad for love of her,

Annie—and in university too: pre-meds. She didn't really care for him—he made her sick with his mooning ways, his bootlicking with her father, and his pretty-faced niceness to her mother. Why, he'd probably be nuts about Laura, clever Laura, a good friend who'd help Annie give the goon the slip—

But Laura wasn't listening to Annie anymore, though she kept on nodding and smiling; she'd caught sight of *him* again, staring at her, and she was desperate to show him that she didn't want his looks any more than she had his note with all its smudged misspellings. Surely it was all a joke, his asking her to come with him on the cruise? Just like the joke that Boris was making now, at the expense of the Golden Boy on top of the parliament building. Everyone was laughing at the mild obscenity: all except Sophie, who'd saved Boris a seat he had declined to take, and who had at last surrendered it to a rapturous Weasel, who had boarded last, without a partner or a place to come to. All except Olga, who had soured her mouth into a frown and complained—more to the back of the seat in front of her than to Stefan—"He should never have been allowed into the seminary. He disgraces his calling. What woman could ever consent to be his wife, to lose all her dignity and position with a *bunyak* like that?" And all except Laura, who was looking out of the window, not at the Golden Boy prancing on the dome, but at the clouds above him and the sky between the clouds: high, hard clouds adrift in windy seas; icebergs seen upside-down, their dense, lead bottoms bruising your eyes, blotting out the airy tops on which angels danced to careless music you could never catch below, however much you tried.

There seemed to be no-one but she, Laura, walking the deck; everyone else was still inside dancing, or helping Boris to open more beer and cheap red wine. One of the oldest students—a swarthy, thick-set, big and stupid guy, immensely popular and nicknamed "the Beast"—had squeezed a laugh like a pimple at the sight of Boris and the booze, but Boris had stood straight up, spread his hands in blessing over them all and chanted, "Do as I say, not as I do." Upon which everyone had cheered, except for Stefan and Olga, who had disappeared, separately, though they all knew them to be meeting somewhere; and Laura, who had been throwing hopeless, worried looks at Annie, who was flirting viciously with George over by the record player, while Lyuba sulked and clamped George's fingers in both her fat, pink palms. George was taking a turn manning the music: when Boris yelled for another record, George had shaken Lyuba off, slapped "Crying in the Chapel" on the turntable, whirled Annie round like a top and escaped with her to the centre of the floor. The lights were already down; dancers hugged the space, wallflowers sagged at the edges of the room, Lyuba sighed and got herself a beer, and Sophie waited at a little table full of untouched sandwiches she'd made in order to be seen to share responsibility for the night with Boris.

Why wouldn't he come to her? He was chaffing George and Annie as they cleaved together and Elvis ullulated; it was Sophie's favourite song, and she prayed he'd hurry up so that they could dance at least a bit of the end together. For after they were married they wouldn't be able to dance as a couple: priests just didn't, even if their wives sometimes did. And she wondered briefly about the priest's wife back home at Dauphin: she came to all the dances with her long yellow hair scrolled at the back of her head (everyone said she dyed it) and her eyelids powdered the colour of the summer sky; no—better than that: the colour of the painted sky inside the church dome, or the blue around the centre of the great Eye of God, staring down at you. Just like the glass eye of the bishop. He had been at the cathedral last Sunday, saying Mass; he had been in a Russian camp, they said, and lost his eye escaping. They also said he'd had his wife put

away so that he could become a bishop. She didn't know—
she couldn't believe that; she might even ask Boris if it were
true. He knew almost everything, he was so clever he would
surely be given a parish in Winnipeg or Saskatoon. They
wouldn't be stuck in Flin Flon or Dauphin all their lives;
they'd get a beautiful house and she would be so kind and
good if only he would at least talk to her, make a sign so
they could fix it for him to come up to her room after the
cruise, the way they always fixed it for Saturday nights. He
was only acting like this to distract attention, suspicion, for
it was true they hadn't behaved as they ought, the way that
Stefan and Olga did. Those two acted as if the whole world
were church, as if God's Eye were spying from every ceiling,
even in the dark. Sophie couldn't believe that either, though
she sometimes wished the priests would talk about God's
Ear, and not his Eye. How could you pray to an eyeball,
however blue—how could it accept your confessions, apolo-
gies, promises? Sophie squeezed her eyes shut, thinking
about Boris' big hands under the covers of her bed, those
Saturday nights. She made tight fists and began to pray:
"Angel of God, my holy guardian, appointed by God for my
protection, I beseech thee: enlighten me this day and protect
me from evil; help me to do good and show me the road to
salvation and please, please, please make him give me the
ring like he promised, please...."

And Laura was all alone on the lower deck, or at least the
only one walking, for she knew that couples were clinched
behind lifeboats, huddled in unlocked cabins. As long as
there was no-one following her, as long as she'd left the
Beast behind. She hated him: he made her want to howl—if
anyone should find out that he was after her she would die.
And why should he want her of all the others—she with her
English mother and her father who'd changed their name
from Martiniuk to Martyn—Laura Martyn—he'd cleverly
put a "y" there as a pivot, so that his daughter could wheel
about from one identity, one language, to another and be at

home in neither. She would never speak Ukrainian as the rest of them did—she couldn't make the letters or the sounds right; she couldn't put the words together. She could only recite what she'd memorized in panic from the grammar book, so that she carried off the examination prize, the diplomas to hang on the walls of her father's study while she couldn't make herself understood to the college cooks, or follow the whisperings of her friends whenever they said things they hoped would sound shameful, things about their bodies or their boyfriends. Even the Beast spoke perfect Ukrainian—out of that slippery, sloppy mouth came pure sounds, true accents. What if she were to go out with him, dance with him tonight—what would she do when he tried to kiss her? How, exactly, did people kiss on the mouth—wouldn't their noses ram together when they smacked lips?

She stopped at the stern, ready to round it and start again, except that she saw them hiding behind an awning—they moved slightly, so that she recognized them this time: sharp, tall, stringy Stefan with his heavy glasses and his face bruised with tenderness; short, stretched Olga who, though his arm was around her, seemed to be standing alone, looking right through the clouds that covered the moon. Stefan was speaking softly in Ukrainian, so that Laura couldn't make out the sense of his words, just their tone—somewhere between delight and fear. But of course she knew that when Olga came back to the dance she'd be wearing under her short white gloves a ring set with a glassy stone. She wondered how Olga could stand there like that—so straight and sure and powerful. But then, Olga was a dancer, she taught them all folkdancing in the college basement to make herself a bit of money for the winter—Annie had told her. She remembered how, the first day of summer-school, she'd watched Olga's mother carrying a suitcase to the dormitory, up three flights of stairs. The mother had been even shorter than her daughter, bowed like a barrel, with a dull kerchief muffling the shape of her head.

And without a face, since she never looked up at all—just followed the click of her daughter's heels. They had not embraced when it was time for the old woman to go—there had just been an exchange of looks at oblique angles: Olga's mother looking down at her daughter's new shoes, Olga looking up at the shell of her mother's face, as if learning the very bones by heart, an icon of what she refused to become. Laura hadn't known that anyone's mother could look like that, like the babas you sometimes saw downtown, bandaged in kerchiefs and aprons, sitting toothless in stockinged feet on small verandahs, peeling potatoes or beets or just shaking their heads and grimacing. Olga wouldn't have that to be afraid of, anymore; she'd be a priest's wife, and that, for a woman, was almost as good as being God's mother. "More honourable than the Cherubim; and beyond compare more glorious than the Seraphim."

Laura turned away, going back along the deck to where music brayed. She was staring at the sky and so managed to trip over the Weasel, who was bending down after something that had fallen by the railing, catching whatever light shone from the smothered moon and the watchlights by the stairs. She jumped with the shock: "Jesus, Weasel, can't you even watch where you're going—tripping me up like that?" He straightened up, pocketing the lie as he always did, and asked her if she'd been hurt. She felt ashamed then, and wanted to say something nice to him, but only made him flush by asking if he were having a good time. He didn't answer, but held up a finger in warning. "The Beast isn't," he said. "He's looking everywhere for you." She said, "Thanks, Weasel," and left him to patter away with his find, which he kept shifting from one hand to the other as he went along. She thought she would go back to the dance—perhaps the Beast wouldn't expect to find her there. And she couldn't keep making the tour of the deck—it was cold; there was only a polished darkness where the moon should have been.

The lights were still low, and a sick-cow crooning came from the record-player as couples, glued shirt-to-blouse, haunch to hip, were dancing standing-still, making eddies in the swamp of heat and smoke and booze. She felt hungry, and was reaching for a sandwich when she saw Sophie crying into the egg-salad, drowning the parched Wonderbread splayed across the platter. "Sophie?" she called—but there was no response, just the same soundless, ceaseless crying, so Laura moved away and began to circle the dance floor. She could recognize no-one in the dark except Lyuba with her hair come all uncurled and her eyes frying in the fat of her face, Lyuba dancing by herself in the middle of the floor. She would hug herself and then reach out her arms to no-one, in sad, slow measure as the record bumped around broken hearts and lost love, the betrayal of earthly perfection, everything that rhymed with blue and true. Lyuba danced it all, drenched strands of hair inking her forehead, the waistband of her dirndl skirt clutching her tighter than any partner ever would.

He hauled her by the wrists onto the dance floor; she kept pushing with stiff arms to keep a space between herself and the Beast, but he was too strong. He crushed her against him and his hands began the continental drift, moving from her shoulders to the small of her back, along the islands of her vertebrae, down to her hips, a castaway, when the music gave a fatal whine and he released her, as ritual decreed, until another record could be chosen. There was just time for her to whirl and run: she reached the steps to the upper deck and knew that he had lost her, wedged in as he was by his gross thickness among the dancers. And so she climbed the stairs and stopped her running, relaxing into the certainty that she was finally alone, cued by the sky into which she could look at last, the moon pure, beaten flat and thin and smooth, slipping in and out of clouds that had worn themselves to rags trying to hold it under. It rubbed the riverbank and the boat; everything magnified and reflected it except for the water below, slicing the light into shivers as the engines thrummed. She leaned over the railing, holding out arms and face to the light of this moon, oblivious of the sound of a latch drawn on the door of the purser's cabin; of the two of them sliding round the slowly opening door— George fastening his belt, Annie buttoning up the waist of the pink-and-purple dress whose paleness seemed roughened by the moonlight. George went down the stairway first; Annie hung back, straightening her dress and her hair, assuming her customary control so that even when she turned and saw Laura standing there, watching the light on the water, she didn't fidget an excuse but staged a little show of concern. Why on earth was Laura mooning about up here when she'd been looking for her everywhere? Laura, jolted by the words, could answer nothing, only stare at the ferocity of joy on Annie's face, knowing at last that Annie had got what she wanted, though why she wanted George so badly Laura would never understand. Tomorrow she would have to listen to all of Annie's griefs against him: his small-ness, his meanness, his failure of a family—all the reasons for which he took her and used her, dropped her and took her up again. All the reasons she set herself to want him, she, the doctor's pink and pretty daughter. But now Annie wanted Laura's silent company, a dull reflection of her brazen shine to walk arm-in-arm back to the dancing, proof of clean hands, cold heart.

This one time Laura didn't care for Annie's jeers or sulks; she let her clump crossly down the stairs, alone. Let her go, let her go, sang the moon; Annie couldn't hurt her now, as long as she stayed here alone and free—free of them all. It was like that part of the Litany she'd sung in choir: "We who mystically represent the Cherubim, let us throw all worldly cares away." If you could stay here long enough alone you might hear the music that the angels make; the notes would slip off the moon like the peel of some great, globed fruit pared round and round by a silver knife. It was

84

getting late; the moon glinted harder, colder, shielding her from the noise steaming up from below. She listened, eyes squeezed shut, but all she heard was the silence of the engines stopping while the gears jumped over to reverse the boat, sending it back downstream. And on the heels of that silence, the grunt of heavy feet up the stairs: the Beast opening beery arms and lowering in front of her.

First she saw the black hairs frizzling his throat and chest beneath the shirt he'd undone in the dancing's heat; then, the helpless clumsiness of his hands as he laid them on the railing, close to hers.

"Pretty night," he said, rocking a little on his heels. "Annie told me you were up here. Yeah, really pretty. Just like you. Pretty yellow hair and big, blue eyes."

Was he making fun of her? Anyone could tell that her hair wasn't blond but mouse-brown; that her eyes were small, narrow, a muddle of grey and green. She wondered at his face: he looked lonely and stupid and wanting something—not her, Laura, but some blind outline, the heroine of some drunken dream-song with whom he'd carelessly matched her. Whatever could she give him to make him go away? She looked straight up into the moon, but the moon was gone—the clouds had swallowed and stomached her. She looked back at the Beast: his mouth was pursed like a baby's, turned up for something sweet, some candy kindness. His fingers were on hers now, hot as sausages in a frying-pan; she couldn't think of what to do except what she always did when she felt hopeless, the way he looked now: to tell herself a story.

She wasn't who he thought she was. Her name was not Laura Martyn. She was not even Ukrainian—nor Canadian —but an orphan, a bareback rider from a wandering circus, a star, a bird under a bad enchantment: anything but what she seemed to be. If he would only let her go now, she would mount the steps up into the moon and disappear—just like that, like a silver coin thrown into a dark river. He let go her hands and listened, his mouth quivering, expectant, as if he really were a hungry baby waiting to be fed; as the bright, thin thread of her storytelling spooled around the doll he'd tried to grab and kiss and cuddle in the dark. Bits of electric light broke off from the boat and splashed on the water; the boat kept chugging downstream, tugged by the city lights you could see now, holding out stubby arms to them. Suddenly there was a bang of doors and a clatter up the stairs. It was Boris—he'd been pitching empties over the side of the boat, and had heard their voices here. He made a clucking noise with his tongue and ordered them downstairs in a voice that was starting to see-saw with tiredness.

All the lights had been flooded onto the dance floor. George had put a *hopak* on the record-player and Stefan was urging everyone into a circle: the wallflowers at the borders of the room, the beer sots, the necking couples from their dim, dumb corners—all joined hands to make a ring through which the real dancers broke by turns. The music rushed so fast it blurred in their ears as dancers split sideways, leaping, spinning arms and legs, spurting from their heels as the girls stamped time, holding out arms like wreaths, coaxing and then refusing the men who hunkered down to them, squatting, sweating, plying haunches, hurling themselves at last into a tight circle—the girls perched now on their linked arms, screaming laughter, throwing back their heads as the others clapped and hooted and stamped in the outer ring. Everyone was there: Stefan and Olga, he clapping his hands with extravagant joy, she, the best dancer among the girls, just letting her toes tap and her calves tense—for a priest's wife does not dance, no matter what Sophie said they did in Flin Flon. Sophie was wedged between Laura and the Beast; the Weasel, darting in and out the ring of watchers, came close enough to see how Sophie's hands slapped mechanically together, out of rhythm, how her eyes bulged with tears. The music was weaving them together, faster and tighter, whirling the dancers faster,

faster, till you could hardly see—and then clicked into abrupt exhaustion. Before they could separate or scatter, Boris was there, rounding them up, ordering them out to the gangway and the quay where their bus was already waiting.

Laura found a place alone in the middle of the bus from which she could just make out the Beast's black, curly head rolling into sleep several seats ahead. Lyuba lubbered on board only to collapse in the seat next to Laura, groaning that she felt sick, feverish; that the exhaust fumes were sure to make her retch. Annie and George were kissing covertly in the seats that Olga and Stefan had taken on the ride down. Those two sat together openly now at the very front of the bus, Stefan's arm stiff as a life preserver round Olga's shoulders. And Boris stood up, perfectly professional beside the driver: counting heads, cracking jokes, winking at everyone save Sophie, who huddled alone in a corner at the extreme back of the bus. Alone except for Weasel, who was shielding her from everyone else's view, and who fingered in his pocket that twist of metal he had retrieved from the boat. You would have thought it was gold, the way it had shone under the lamps—unless you'd seen the dark spots splotching the strands of the true-lovers' knot. Sophie had given that ring to Boris at the summer's beginning, the Weasel knew. From the shadow of an awning he had watched Boris fish the ring from the pocket of his black serge trousers, hand it back to Sophie, saying how sorry he was. He was going off to Regina the next day, back to a wonderful girl he'd known for a long time, a friend of the family to whom he'd been more or less engaged for the last year, though he was awfully fond of Sophie who was such a good sport, none better. The Weasel had been sure Sophie would grab back that ring, scratch it out of Boris' fingers and hurl it deep down into the river, but she hadn't. She'd just put her hand out for it, like it was Communion bread—not even knowing it was slipping through her fingers, down between the planks that he was memorizing from his hiding place.

Sophie didn't even know that he was sitting beside her here. She was all null and blotted—like a mirror without any images to catch and keep. The bus had pulled into the college parking-lot, was almost empty when he put his hand on hers. She started at the damp, cool twitch of his fingers on her skin; gave a short, sick cry, as if it were a severed hand she were pushing away. And then she lurched to her feet and looked straight through him, her mouth so wide he thought her lips must tear, though no words came. Until she started to scream in the emptied bus:

"Oh God, God, how could you? You liar, you filthy, rotten liar, you louse—oh my God I hate you, I hate you—you, you, you...." The rest in a squeal of shame: "You, Weasel? You?"

He waited till she had stumped away, almost like a cripple, down the aisle of the bus. When he was alone he took out the ring and, cushioning it against his palm, stroked it tenderly, even the dark places where the gold had gone. He had to hurry: it would soon be time for Evening Prayers, and he was serving as altar boy this night, wearing the silver robes over his stunted arms and legs. With Stefan and Boris he would chant solemn words, sad sounds—he began to repeat them now, to the ceiling of the bus:

> Have mercy, O Lord, upon us sinners devoid of all defence. Be not wroth with us, neither remember our iniquities, but look down on us in mercy as thou art our God and we are thy people; we are all the work of thy hand, and we call upon thy Name.

"*My* name—" he whispered to the silence that still quavered with Sophie's scream. "My name is Andrei."

Mrs. Mucharski & the Princess

"Pretty lady have pretty baby," were Mrs. Mucharski's first words to Laurie on her triumphal return from the hospital. They seemed to print the necessary ceremonial flourish over the confused joy of the occasion, shaping the moment as delicately and permanently as the pink kid-leather frames in which Vic, a few weeks later, enclosed the first photographs of Laurie and the baby on the hospital steps.

It was not only that she had spoken perfect truths—for neither camera nor film could make out mother and daughter as anything other than pretty figures in pretty-coloured clothes—but also that Mrs. Mucharski's accent had somehow rarefied the triteness of the compliment, so that she seemed to be performing an incantation or rendering some magical phrase out of an old folksong. R's trilled, a's lolled, v's huffed; together they summoned images from opulently illustrated editions of Russian fairy-tales. Laurie assumed that the housekeeper, with her Slavic cheekbones and tongue, had issued from the Eastern European hodge-podge: Czech, Bulgarian, Polish, Ukrainian, Hungarian— it didn't much matter which. She was foreign and intricately so, independent from her employers both in the shape and tone of her speech, so that when Mrs. Mucharski spoke it was, for all her drab clothes and spare face—which had certainly never been pretty—as if she were addressing her equals.

Perhaps, Sheila had hinted, the woman was an ex-princess or at least of noble blood, fallen from good fortune after some natural or historical disaster, and forced to work for her bread like a hard-luck heroine in a fairy-tale. It had been Sheila, ever the indispensable sister-in-law (married for the second time to a Lebanese computer-salesman who claimed descent from a royal house) who had suggested Mrs. Mucharski when the pediatric nurse the agency had engaged fell through.

"It's a blessing in disguise, Laurie," Sheila had urged. "Whatever do you want a nurse for—you can manage all the care for the baby yourself, that's child's play" (Sheila had four of her own) "as long as you've got help in the house. You know, for cooking, cleaning, laundry, all the drudge work. And Mrs. Mucharski's a gem—a pearl, positive. She's not just a peasant from off the boat, with sweaty armpits and a moustache: she's a lady. And she's honest as the day—of how many Portuguese or Vietnamese people can you say that? She *works,* she doesn't just laze around and chitter-chatter. And she's not expensive, either, especially compared with what you'd have to pay for a pediatric nurse—"

The money, Laurie had interrupted, would be no problem. Vic insisted on the best, and, as Sheila would know, he could afford to get it. This was not just random bitchery; Laurie had, more than a trifle guiltily, wanted someone who could look after the prospective baby for a few hours every day, so that she could escape downtown once in a while; shop, meet friends for lunch, unwind and unbond a bit after her pregnancy. Sheila would have clucked at this, nattered about La Lèche (she still had a two year old tugging at her breasts) and how money was just no substitute for mother-love—so Laurie had deflected her by lighting a little flare of sibling rivalry and had then pounced with: "But if this Mrs. Mucharski is so good, then why isn't she registered with one of the big agencies? It's not that I don't trust your judgment, Sheila, but after all, where a newborn baby is concerned...."

"That's not her style," Sheila had squealed. "She's a classy housekeeper, believe me; she likes people to come to her— and she's choosy. Look, Laurie, she may not *want* to work for you at all: *she* doesn't need the best that money can buy. Some of us plain poor people make do very well without— oh, what the hell, I want to help you out. She's not with an agency, I guess, because—I've never asked her straight out, she's not that type of person—because there might be some slight problem with immigration." Here Sheila's voice had gone all sweet and snaky through the telephone coils. "Not that there's anything fishy—she's straight as a ruler, is Mrs. Mucharski, and she's been in Canada—oh, for years and years, but—well, it seems that she just never did the proper bureaucratic things when she arrived—you know, all that kaboodle with red and pink and blue tape. Besides, she's sensitive about her age—I mean, God knows how old she is, you can't just tot her up as if she were rouged to the hilt and dyed her hair gentian violet. Fifty-five, sixty-five— who knows? But she can do things, Laurie; why, you'll be just astounded"—Sheila blew the vowels of the word in and out as if they were a blob of bubblegum—"at the things she'll do for you."

And so she'd come—the very day after Vic had driven a carefully breathing Laurie into the maternity hospital—and stayed. By the time Vic had brought Laurie home, Mrs. Mucharski had transcended Sheila's gushes. It was not an easy house to care for, Laurie had run through a baker's dozen of different cleaning women in the year they'd lived there, and all of them put together hadn't managed to accomplish what Mrs. Mucharski had in that one week. Walls had been washed, curtains brushed, even mending attended to: the heap of scarcely worn clothing Laurie had thrown into a cardboard box to give to St.-Vincent de Paul had all been sorted, salvaged and put neatly into drawers.

The ivory-and-turquoise Chinese carpets had not merely been vacuumed, but first washed, combed and plumed somehow, so that you'd swear no-one ever could have walked on them. If you could work enchantments with linseed oil and flannel cloths, Ajax and Windex and bleach, then Mrs. Mucharski was some sort of good fairy out of a story book, though with her humped fingers and hooked back she looked much more like a wicked witch, webbed in by some white magic. Perhaps this would explain why, after nursing the baby (for at the eleventh hour Laurie had been converted by La Lèche) and putting her down to sleep in the wicker basinette that had once been her own, Laurie should feel Mrs. Mucharski's sharply angled face and grave, strange voice shuttle in and out the weave of her own dreams, that first night home.

2

During the first week of Mrs. Mucharski's stay Laurie held court in the mid-mornings and late afternoons. Neighbours, acquaintances from the pre-natal classes she'd attended, friends from work, themselves either babyless or unremarried or both, would stop by to see the baby and to gossip with Laurie in her upstairs sitting-room, dabbling stockinged toes in the plush ivory carpeting, sipping hot, fragrant teas out of porcelain cups, tearing large bites out of the breads and cakes and buns with which the housekeeper had laden the tea tray. For ever since Mrs. Mucharski's arrival the kitchen air had hummed with the warm spice of baking: poppy-seed strudels, shining braids of golden bread, small pastries plumped with cheese or meat crowded each other on the larder shelves. And as they watched the crooked, neat, old woman come and go, her eyes never meeting any curious glance, her hair braided into a tight steel-coloured band across the top of her head, Laurie's visitors would nod their heads and whisper about the treasure she had found, and then about her good luck in general. Such a baby, such a husband, such a house, such a housekeeper, what fabulous luck: she was like some princess at the end of a fairy-tale. But Laurie would only laugh, or smile and shake her head so that her lovely hair fell into her great, coffee-coloured eyes. And if, in her fluted tea-gown, with her peaceful, basinetted baby and her sitting-room jungling with hot-house flowers she was complacent in her happiness, who could blame her? For what is happiness but a talent for luxuriating in your own given circumstances: circumstances which, Laurie's whole attitude declared, had flocked to her as naturally as birds to a broad-branched tree at evening.

So there she sat on top of her kingdom, like a candied cherry on a peak of flushed meringue, while those of her friends who'd brought their babies scorched their tongues on her tea, remembering their entropic houses heaped with unwashed, milk-stiff nightgowns and souring baby things, while their own infants fretted, mewled, popped out in nervous rashes and spat up over their shabby jeans. And the bare-wombed ex-colleagues from the small, expensive shop for which Laurie had been a buyer cooed over the baby's bonnets and smocked nightdresses, and told Laurie that she looked like an ad for Ivory Snow. And Laurie just looked prettily down at the reflection quivering in her full tea-cup, or rang the brass bell for Mrs. Mucharski to come up the stairs with a fresh pot or another plate of delicious things for her guests.

At last, however, everyone who could possibly want to see the baby had come and gone, without ever following up on their promises to return, or to invite Laurie to their own, less happy houses. Only Sheila kept dropping by, with two or more of her over-fed, contrary children and warnings about how this honeymoon phase of newborn bliss would last no longer than a pair of stockings. After four such visits Laurie instructed Mrs. Mucharski to tell Sheila that she was resting any time she called, or that the doctor had forbidden visits from anyone with small, snuffling children. And the housekeeper, for all that Sheila had been her good angel in getting her this job, did just as she was told. Somewhat nonplussed, Laurie added this to the list of things she was finding out about Mrs. Mucharski: that her loyalties were strictly professional and temporary, like the jobs she did.

She actually knew very little about the woman, in spite of the fact that, as her visitors failed and the weather tapered into endless fine, autumnal rain, Laurie spent all her days indoors with only the housekeeper and an increasingly wakeful baby to distract her. One afternoon she'd sat rocking her daughter in a pale blue-velvet chair, watching Mrs. Mucharski expertly unhook, wash and polish the prisms of the Orrefors chandelier that Vic had brought back from his last business trip abroad. She noticed how the woman's eyes tightened each time she picked up a fragment of the crystal, so clear and slippery-cool it seemed to turn to water in her hands. She saw the small, purplish mole above Mrs. Mucharski's left eyebrow quiver as she knit her forehead at

94

her work; she noticed how her lips seemed to make involuntary tremblings, as if she were praying to herself. Laurie asked various unpatterned questions that were answered as tersely as possible.

"Have you any children, Mrs. Mucharski?"

"No."

"Is your husband living?"

"No."

"What country do you come from?"

"I Canadian, now. Canada my country."

"Have you lived here long?"

"Yes."

And finally, with more irritation than concern, "Mrs. Mucharski, you work too hard—don't you ever sit down and rest for a bit? Sit down now and relax, and just let yourself be for a minute." But the woman had kept her silence until, having reassembled the chandelier and skillfully re-hung it, she turned to Laurie, saying in the odd, encrusted accent, "No, lady. Once I be sit down do nothing, I start think, start and no finish. And then I be finish, too." She'd looked Laurie in the eyes with her own—not large, not beautiful but precise, judging eyes that rode the slant of her cheekbones, lodging in her face the way a night light settles into a room, illuminating odd patches of ceiling, throwing up soft, distorted shadows. And though Laurie had been opening her mouth to say something, Mrs. Mucharski turned away from her, taking her polishing cloths and the small stepladder on which she had been standing, leaving Laurie to the darkening ruin of the afternoon.

3

Whatever it was Mrs. Mucharski refused to let herself think, Laurie wasn't likely to find out. It had happened at any rate, over there, in that country the housekeeper would not name, that place where history went on—real history, the kind that was someone else's nightmare. When Laurie talked with a certain kind of stranger—hairdressers, or cleaning ladies—she wanted small, clear, coloured bits of information about their lives, certainly no black pools that might muddy her own bright reflection.

Once or twice, perhaps, she had wondered what it would be like to have everything you possessed wrenched from you, as she supposed had happened to Mrs. Mucharski all those years ago. House, family, even your language—all gone, for good. But she hadn't a very generous imagination, it stretched no larger than the soft warm smallness of her own skin. Mrs. Mucharski would not talk, Laurie would ask no more questions, and their silence would be a clean, snowy Switzerland between them, permitting a sure neutrality of emotion. For Mrs. Mucharski no more demanded pity from anyone than she exercised grudges against those who possessed what she presumably had lost. She went about her endless, infinitesimal tasks with the impersonal fidelity of a verger in some large church. While Laurie flitted in and out of the rooms of her house, the woman kept to her work: the cleaning, baking, polishing and putting-away that sent a hum of well-tempered domesticity through the household air. And if Mrs. Mucharski never asked to hold or rock the baby; if she never stopped over the basinette to watch the ferocious soundness of her sleep or to place a finger in the passionate grip of the baby's toylike hand, it was, perhaps, only that never having had children she didn't like babies. Lots of people were like that; Laurie didn't mind.

So that when things started to go wrong it wasn't as if Mrs. Mucharski had somehow witched the house, disordering the baby's routine or souring Laurie's milk. Yet it was at her that Laurie snapped one morning when, with nothing to look forward to all day but a baby to feed and change and bathe, she had lain spread-eagled over the brass-bound double bed, pressing reddened eyes into the comforter. Her stitches still twitched painfully when she bent down, her belly hadn't yet lost its pregnant puffiness, and her breasts, which once had been as small and snowy as apples, were now long, darkened with railroading veins, the nipples puckered. They hurt her as she hiccoughed short, hard sobs, and then they began to leak warm driblets of milk through the cups of her nursing brassiere, past her peignoir and into the comforter. Sitting up, she fished her reflection from the floor-length mirror that hung across the wall from the bed. She wanted other images, that easy icon of new motherhood that had been beamed at her from every magazine cover, every ad for baby oil: some sixteen-year-old model simulating maternity with a downy-diapered baby who would toddle off and let her be once the photography was finished. To be fresh, untouched, still virgin, somehow; free to create and float appearances without always that anchor of small, vulnerable, all-demanding flesh she'd thought to have shed as she had the rubber plate of after-birth in the delivery-room.

All the mirror gave her back was her own blubbered face, the damp patches making twin bull's-eyes of her breasts, and—Mrs. Mucharski's slight, hooked figure, laden now with armfuls of floaty stuff resembling clouds that had spun through rainbows. "Lady," she was saying, "lady, your things, I be washing two, three times, try clean...." The flounced and ribboned things were the nightgowns Laurie'd taken into hospital with her—stupidly, for they'd all been scarred by ugly thick stains from the blood clots and discharge she had passed after the birth. She flushed and took the things from Mrs. Mucharski's arms, she crammed them into an open drawer and shoved it shut, ripping one of the peignoirs as she did so. It shamed her to have had this old woman handle her things, her very blood. To have had her see her things unclean like that was an intimacy she could not bear, and so she turned petulant, shouting, "Get out, go away—and leave my things alone. I don't want you to touch my things ever again; do you understand?"

Mrs. Mucharski nodded, but her eyes seemed to hook into Laurie's face; when she walked out she left a mustiness of disapproval behind. Laurie stood up, and threw a pillow at the shadows the old woman had made. Why should that sour-faced witch be judging her with those small, hard eyes? Who did she think she was—whose house did she think this was? And she pushed her head into the comforter again, choking on her sobs; it was all Mrs. Mucharski's fault; if they had got the nurse, the lady the agency had lined up for them, she would be free now, she'd have someone with whom to leave the baby—she could go out, downtown, see her friends, live as she'd used to.... She would show them all: she'd wean the baby, fire Mrs. Mucharski, hire a proper nurse....

But then the house would fall to pieces, and Vic would complain; and the baby was hers—she didn't want to give it up to some paid stranger. So Laurie had risen from the bed, washed her face, dressed, and taken the baby outside, avoiding Mrs. Mucharski as if the woman really were a witch who'd walked into their house from some ogre-ridden fairy-tale instead of from the city bus. Jumpy, nervy, she found it difficult to push the high-wheeled, bouncy carriage straight along the sidewalk. Instead of lying back like a little oyster in a flounced shell the baby whimpered, screw-faced, in the frilled sleeping-suit Laurie had dressed her in. Above her head the baggy clouds kept threatening rain; she saw a few steel pins dance off the hood of the baby-carriage and so she turned back in the direction of her house. Never before had she felt quite so leaden at the thought of reaching her front steps, the fluted columns, the fake Georgian portico, the glossy shutters that were nailed against the brick and which, even if they could have moved, would never have shut flush together. All those were not even unique in their prosperous pretence: every fourth house along the new-developed block had features parallel, and just as false. They'd moved here because of the baby—Vic wanted three children close together—because of the baby, this baby crying raucously as Laurie fumbled with the catch of the carriage hood, getting the lace of the sleeping-suit entangled with the wing-bolt in the process. Incompetent, useless—she wouldn't have made it even as a nanny, she despaired, feeling the hot prick of tears under her eyelids. At last she got the baby free, just as the rain gushed down.

It seemed as if her key unlocked some stranger's house; the reflections of newly polished brass and copper, the pristine arrangement of the furniture threw foreign gleams and shadows over her memory of how things used to be inside the house—her house—before Mrs. Mucharski had arrived. Everything had changed so—the breezy calm with which she'd first assumed responsibility for the baby while in hospital, the regal control she had assumed to have over the running of the house. Such unexplained, disastrous differences—what could these be but a counter-spell to her accustomed happiness, her certain luck? This would be the reason why the baby, instead of nuzzling blindly toward Laurie's breasts and latching on to the warm jets of milk, had now begun to pull away and squirm, or send up a baffled cry after a few furious sucks. This would explain why, if she did feed well, she would in half-an-hour's time shudder awake, her chin a-quiver and her tiny legs drawn up. Fretting, starting at the least irregular noise, whining unless she were carried up against Laurie's shoulder, her head crooning into the hollow just below the collarbone, the baby had begun to keep poor Laurie up half the night and all the day.

Throughout that first distempered week Vic tried to spell her off and on but he hadn't enough time; he was working late these nights on a big project for which his company had just contracted, and that he couldn't afford to neglect. When Laurie complained of lines and shadows under her eyes, of taut nerves and listless boredom, stuck at home all day and night with a whining baby, he'd barked at her:

99

"What else have you got to do besides look after the baby and yourself? Mrs. Mucharski runs the house, I pay the bills, you nurse the baby. Look, she's not a doll, of course she'll cry some of the time, all you've got to do is mother her, so go on—what are you, unnatural or something?"

Over the telephone the doctor had impatiently collapsed Laurie's inquiries as to baby-tranquillizers as if they were so many tottery bowling-pins. "Colic," he'd diagnosed, "colic pure and simple. It comes on suddenly like that, in the third or fourth week—it'll last maybe two or three months and then disappear as magically as it came. You'll just have to cope—the way your mother did with you, and hers with her. Get a sitter in, from time to time, to give yourself a break." But Vic's reproach had armoured Laurie; when he'd returned one lunchtime from yet another business trip, with a dozen cream-coloured roses, tickets to a play and an offer from Sheila to babysit if they couldn't engage a sitter from the agency, Laurie had hurled the roses at him, thorns and all, and locked herself into the bathroom of the master bedroom while Vic explained the intricacies of post-partum depression through the keyhole. And all the time the baby kept up a siren-wail of discontent, until Vic had had to break off his suasions and go pace the upper landing to a slow, womb-tempo with his fractious daughter in his arms and his wife sobbing into the dry Jacuzzi at the hopelessness of it all: what sitter would be able to stand more than half an hour of that unceasing, plangent misery? Finally Vic had paced the child to silence and put her delicately into the basinette, terrified of shattering the fragile shell of her sleep. And then he'd padded down the stairs, closed the front door silently behind him and returned an hour later with a year's hoard of Similac in the back of the car.

Perhaps it was because he advanced upon her with a tin and bottle opener as if they were a bayonet that Laurie shouted when she really could have laughed; perhaps it was because she'd hardly slept the night before that she grabbed the Similac out of her husband's hands and threw it at the ceramic tiles of their bathroom floor, from where it bounced up into the giant mirror over the vanity, slashing it into a hundred scintillant ribbons. And then they both began to scream, so single-mindedly that neither heard the baby waking up and joining in.

"How dare you! How dare you interfere with the way I nurse my baby! She's *mine* to feed; I have nothing else to do, remember? You leave us alone—"

"Leave you alone to starve her? What kind of a mother are you if you don't even know your baby's starving? The doctor—"

"Screw the doctor—he wouldn't even come and look at—"

"Of course he wouldn't pay a house call just to hold the hand of some spoiled suburban—"

"You're the one—you're the one who wanted to come to these stupid suburbs. Remember those three kids you wanted to have, 'close together'?"

"I remember—and I wish right now that we'd never...."

"Don't say it, don't, Vic."

As is the way of such things, they'd frightened each other into arms so tight and quick they almost squeezed themselves breathless. Laurie made little, whimpering sounds as Vic kissed the top of her head and the quivering domes of her eyelids, and it was another ten minutes before either was quiet enough for Vic to loose his arms and say, "We'd better get Mrs. Mucharski in to sweep up all that glass...."

But when they looked for her Mrs. Mucharski was nowhere to be found—neither in the kitchen, nor in the laundry-room, nor in the slightly stuffy, somewhat damp bedroom that had been prepared for her in the basement of the house. Suddenly terrified, Laurie gripped her husband's arm and whispered, "Vic—oh, Vic—the baby? What if she's gone, and kidnapped the baby? It's been known to happen—and she never liked the poor little thing, and—"

Vic told her not to be an idiot, but, all the same, he raced ahead of her up the stairs to the top floor where the baby had her small and separate room. They opened the door, but froze on the threshold like a pair of children discovered in flagrant misdeed. For there, in the old, curly-maple platform rocker that Vic had had specially refinished for his wife, sat Mrs. Mucharski, her steel-coloured hair woven into a tight crown upon her head, her sturdy, shabby shoes rooted deeply in the carpet-fluff, her fine, hard eyes enclosing the face of their little daughter, to whom she was feeding milk out of a baby-bottle, while chanting some low, deep song that had no words, just a soothing throb: ay-yah-ah; ay-yah-ah. And it was not until the whole bottle had been finished, and the baby's eyes were closing in a gassy smile at some bright image on the undersides of her eyelids that Mrs. Mucharski rose, brought the baby over to Laurie's limp arms and surrendered her, saying, "This baby hungry; be cry, no can sleep." And she walked more in stateliness than arrogance away from them, down the corridor and stairs to some empty portion of the house.

When Vic had showered—after picking up the slivered glass off the ceramic tiles—and dressed, and returned to work; when Laurie had bathed, penitently dressed in one of the few matronly smocks she possessed, and come downstairs to the kitchen, it seemed as if nothing had really happened. Mrs. Mucharski was at the worktable, kneading dough. Laurie listened to the sounds of the woman's hands slapping and shaping the pale damp-looking mass. Then, angry at her own awkwardness, she walked a little too quickly to Mrs. Mucharski's side, so that she bumped into the table, and caused the woman to leave off her kneading for a moment, just to absorb the shock. Into that freed space, Laurie plunged.

"She was hungry; she's sleeping beautifully now. I guess I haven't enough milk of my own for her. They say that often happens, when you're upset or tired. The books say that—

you know——?"

"You know nothing."

The words went into Laurie like a bee's sting: barbed, so that each blundering attempt to pull it out only makes new points of pain. That pain was wholly foreign, inexplicable; why should this woman, come in to do the cleaning and thus to spare Laurie fatigue and fuss, possess the power to cause sharp, even if small, suffering? Yet, staring into the woman's face, seeing the way the skin puckered about the eye-sockets, and how her own image gaped in the distorting mirrors of Mrs. Mucharski's eyes, Laurie seemed to be tugging slow words out of flesh that had scarred and hardened over.

"I be having twin babies; girl and boy. I be in camp; no food, no water, nothing; filth everywhere, filth and empty, dead, everything. I be have"—and here she dropped her eyes to the kitchen counter, as if searching for something; she finally picked up a paring knife. "I be skin, bone, no more fat on me than this knife, but I feed my children, I make milk from my body, for giving to my babies—"

She stopped, all of a sudden, as if someone had seized the knife from her and begun to trace her backbone with it. The knife had simply dropped from her hands, which she had involuntarily stretched open as if to feel her way past some obstacle, in some obscurity.

Laurie gave another tug: "What camp, Mrs. Mucharski, where?"

"Far away—not in your country. Labour camp. Prison camp. No understand, lady."

"And your babies, Mrs. Mucharski? What happened to your little girl and boy?" Laurie had to ask, had to determine the facts, had to pull and tug to get free from that first sting. Mrs. Mucharski did not look at her; instead she stopped her kneading and put floury hands up to her head—a gesture that seemed as if it should end in her fastening a strand of hair, but which finished with her putting hands over her ears.

"I have no babies, no babies, none." She looked up at Laurie, still covering her ears. "I have—nothing. You understand, lady, you understand, now?"

And then, as if her throat were a machine-gun she had loaded, which kept spattering long after Laurie had quit the room:

"No babies; none, none, none—"

She told Vic, that night, something of what had happened, but couldn't make him understand what had upset her so. "Poor old woman," he'd said—or something like that. And when, before going to sleep in the big, brass-bound bed, she'd pulled at his arm to say "But, really—you don't think all that happened, do you? It's not true—the way she said it?" he only rubbed her hand briefly, muttering, "How can I tell? Look, it's ancient history, and another lifetime altogether. Besides, it's none of our business. Go to sleep, Laurie, you need your rest."

But before she could get to sleep, Laurie heard the baby crying: she got out of bed without turning on the lights, not wanting to wake her husband. Feeling her way along the corridor and up the stairs she crept to where the night lamp was shining in her baby's room. Carefully, slowly, steadily as she moved, it seemed a long, long way off, that small light at the very end of the landing. As she came nearer, though, it seemed to split into two gleams, two eyes inside a lantern that was no lantern but a skull, a bone cage lengthening link by link into an entire skeleton. It was a woman's skeleton—inside the ribcage were two small, skeleton babies, clinging to the ribs with fingers no thicker than a hair, and nuzzling at the space between the bones. And the skeleton-woman was putting her arms out to Laurie, whether to brace herself against, or to embrace her, she didn't know; for now there were her husband's arms round her instead, and his hands stroking the thick, toffee-coloured hair from her eyes, and his voice saying soothing, comforting things that had no meaning but which made handles for her to grab while she told him her nightmare.

"She's not real, is she? Is she?" Laurie kept repeating, her face pressed into her husband's shoulder. "Because if she is real, then how can I be, too? And in the stories it's the old woman, the witch, who goes up the chimney or dances in red-hot shoes till she dies, so that everyone else can keep on happily, ever-after—" And Vic kept crooning, "Of course not, of course; you're all right, it's just hormones, ancient history—she'll go tomorrow, we don't need her anymore, we'll tell her tomorrow—"

But in the morning it was Mrs. Mucharski who stood in the front hall with her cracked vinyl bag, her eyes impassive as she told them she was leaving. She folded five weeks' wages into her small handbag, refusing Vic's offer of a drive to the bus stop. She would walk, she said—she preferred to walk.

From an upstairs window, holding her baby snug in her arms, Laurie watched Mrs. Mucharski leave the shelter of the porch and walk down the steps, along the sidewalk and round a corner, until she disappeared. The image of her flickered just for a moment, then vanished, as if it had been no more than a blade of shadow on a windy day.

In a Dream

I have had the most extraordinary dream—the kind of dream that takes you, blindfolded, hands tied, down narrow, long, obliquely angled corridors, almost forever. Only to halt and for no reason push you out sleep's door onto that ledge between night and morning, that desolation in which you can feel, see, hear nothing to tell whether you're safe awake or prisoned still inside your sleep. Where sleeping is an inching belly-crawl across split glass, shattered metal; where waking is to find yourself washed after shipwreck to a welcome, opalescent emptiness of shore.

It is because of watching the late news, my husband will say. It comes from letting in those supple, cunningly transmitted images of burning, bursting bodies that the mind calls and the eyes refuse as other people. It is because of reading, in all idle innocence, newsmagazines left out in waiting-rooms: stories of people in far places starved, beaten, buried alive in ice or dumped like refuse into slow, mud-swollen rivers.

It is because of the child thrashing in my belly to be born, my doctor will say. Heavily pregnant women are moody, anxious and sleep poorly, entertaining nightmares as if they were paying guests. It is normal to be fretful, credulous: to watch the late news and scan newspaper stories, saying of the women whose husbands disappear, it could be me; of the children whose small, searching arms, whose unblinking faces have been smashed by bombs, they could be mine. For a pregnant woman—and pregnancy, they say, is a sickness —it is easy to have bad dreams.

In my dream I have woken from soft, dark sleep to listen for the echoes of some danger that has roused me: our daughter has fallen out of bed and hurt herself, and starts to cry, or a thief is padding up the stairs, turning the handle of the bedroom door. The wind, perhaps, has blown open a screen door that bangs against the stillness of the night. Two men in clothes so dark I can make out only their faces, bleary moons above my bed, shove a gun at my heart, just above the taut bulge of my eight-month's-old child.

There is no clumsy thief, no child has tumbled out of bed, no door blown open. I have made them up, my stupid fear has blown them like balloons to bursting point against the bedroom ceiling; they fall in shivers to the floor. The baby has twisted and kicked, somehow, to startle me awake; I can close my eyes again and fit my swollen, softened body into the empty space against my husband's chest, pull his warmth and soundless sleep like a quilt about me until morning, wrap us gently, surely. If it were not for the steel of that finger probing my breastbone for a target. There are two men in dark clothes, pointing a gun at my heart.

They say nothing—they have no need. I know them, have already felt their arms, thick and brute as planks of wood, already watched their white eyes on a television screen, in the pages of a magazine. I lumber out of bed more quickly than if I'd heard my daughter calling out to me; too quickly for a pregnant woman. I understand they will give me no time to dress myself or put shoes on my feet; if I ask questions, make demands, curse or plead they will shove at me with their guns and push me down the stairs. They will threaten to take my husband, too—my husband who is still asleep, his body curving gently, tenderly, toward the space where I lie. They will take him and then who will be there to comfort, to protect our daughter when she wakes in the morning?

I have been good, I have been quiet and obedient, but still they push me downstairs, lash my hands tight together behind my back. Stumbling, I reach the front door that gapes, making a wordless howl like a mouth whose teeth have been smashed to the roots. Was it the noise of their kicking down the door that woke me? Why has no-one else heard, why are there no lights on all the length of this small cul-de-sac on which we live—it is safer for children here, there is no traffic on a cul-de-sac. Only one light on in all these large and surely fastened houses: one neighbour, whose body I see outlined against the lantern of her bare window. It is a woman I know, with her newborn in her arms; she has just finished feeding her baby and is standing at the window, looking at the full moon locked within the mazy branches of a tree. Does she see me, arms lashed behind, belly forced helplessly before me: a straining balloon that the merest clumsy touch, the abruptness of this autumn air, might puncture? Does she see me in this dream of mine, or does she think that she, herself, is dreaming?

I am thrust into the darkness that the opening of the van doors has made. It smells pungent, you can taste salt; it feels like blood tastes, it is like drowning in thick, warm, sour blood as the doors are shut and the engine drags us away. Columns of cramped flesh, invisible to one another, wedged upright—there is no sitting down, there is no space to sit or even move your lips to form the words it is worthless to speak, since you already know where you are going, who the others are, why they are here with you, what will be done to you as the van speeds down the smooth, dead streets and across the city, out of the city to where no-one will ever come to find us.

In the 60 or 100 seconds' worth of lodging that this dream has of my brain I am stripped, even of my nightdress, beaten on the arms I wrap like staves around my belly, pitched onto the slime of my cell floor once, five, twenty, a hundred times. No-one tells me what I may do to stop what they are doing to me, to my child whose only guilt is to be here inside me, unborn and still alive. There is no-one to help me, no help for it, I am their enemy, a willful menace to the sleep of those who rule, and thus I must be removed from sight the way a madman would remove a stain from a cloth: by taking a dull knife and bruising out a hole. I am alone in this cell, with a hundred others alone in theirs: so many rents, so many blood-stuffed gaps, how can it ever hold together? But it does.

How many days, how many hours and minutes have they held me here? I measure out my time in the bowls of slop pushed through my door; the pulping of my fists against that door for the rags with which to wipe up my own excrement; the messages that pass from cell to cell like the skitter of rats' feet, the grating of rats' teeth against steel and cement. My baby deep inside me hears, smells, sees only the warm salt of my blood and water swirling over her as if she were some surely anchored sea anemone. She does not kick so much, now, thrusting against the warm, blind water, working to be born. She knows it is better to wait, to curl herself fiercely inward, make herself small and still within this womb they have begun to hollow the way wasps gut peaches bulging rose and golden on the helpless tree.

And still it holds. My husband and my daughter wake each morning, dress themselves, lie down to sleep each night as if I were still there, as if I had never been. A disappearance is not death but mere erasure; trying to trace the word invisibly pressed into the page will only bring more wakings in the night, more metal fingers prying the heart from bones fear has clenched. I am glad of their silence, their stillness; if I could send them any word from here it would be that they do well and that to do well is to keep out of here. As I tell my baby it is better to keep in the warm, safe, salt-dark unborn. At least they do not put children here: what comes through the cracks and fissures of my cell, voice and breath embittered at their own persistence, is not children's perilous, fierce grief, hurt, hunger. All that I hear is just the news that comes from cell to cell: who has been brought in, worked over, dumped outside. Once, five, twenty, a hundred thousand times....

When I woke this time there was someone with me. I was on a bed—a plank of wood propped on an iron frame. What had been so poorly hid, so treacherously sheltered in me had been forced out at last: another hole ripped in the cloth. The someone with me changed the rags that staunched the blood soaking the wooden plank; dribbled water from a dirty sponge over lips my tongue could scarcely reach, and did not speak. I knew from the scars that once had been the features of her face that she had lain as I lay on a blood-drenched bed, tended by someone who by now would have disappeared for the second time, the last time. I could look at her face only for bursts of time—it was like looking into a dead star: too dull to warm, irradiate enough to blind. I shut my eyes and thought of the other one of mine, the daughter who woke each day and clung to an unravelling safety net. I prayed she would simply stop remembering me, or better, that my husband would teach her to unlearn my ever having been, if that would keep her in the sound spaces of the cloth, hugging the webbing of the net. And praying, too, that I would for the second and last time, be made to disappear.

Whenever I woke, she would be with me. When I was strong enough to lift to my mouth the slop they pushed, twice every day, through the door, she spoke to me. She did not tell her name—that would have been too crude an intimacy. Instead, she told me she would be taken soon— they had forced from her all she could ever give, and there was no-one left outside to plead for her. One out of a thousand who disappeared here went out alive, she said. Sometimes the wife or husband, son or mother who had not been taken in the middle of the night had friends who could make noise to strangers. Sometimes the lost could be found. Not she. They would keep her here a little longer; then they would cut her open with electric needles and dull razors, as if they were skilled surgeons and the patient they were labouring to save, her pain. Then they would put a gun at her breast or the nape of her neck, shoot her a dozen times and dump her in the ground where her husband and a hundred other husbands would already have been made to vanish by the earth and everything that pulses in it. And that those who had been left behind in the city would know of this the way you know a mistake that has been made in writing, a mistake rubbed out so diligently that its very absence becomes a thing you know by heart.

I have been afraid to sleep for fear that she will be taken from me before I wake. Yet I have slept and dreamed I tore the lids off my eyes, to keep awake, to keep her beside me, watching the door that has not opened, hearing the shots that have not come. I have told her that I know she will be killed, and can bear this, but I cannot survive the thought that she will be taken again, taken from me.

She only says that so far they have not brought any children here. I say nothing. We both know they have world and time enough to practise any horror we can think of: that neither our bone nor our brain can make shelters deep and still enough they cannot pierce and loot them.

She knows that they are voiding the cells of old prisoners— that it has been by some perfection of cruelty or neglect she has been left so long with me, giving us this temporary comfort of each other's suffering. "Listen," she motions, and we bend our heads down to the grate from which come sounds so muffled, dexterous and hateful they might be rats' feet, rats' teeth tunnelling. For each of us in every cell there is only this one message: now they are coming for you, coming. Long before we hear the tramp of boots in our corridor we know. So that we have the time—a moment—for something more desirable than a word or embrace: the sharing of what we, together, know.

When they come I am crouched on the plank of my bed, behind the door, my eyes blanked by the knees I have drawn up and am pressing into eyesockets, so that I will not have to see. But I do. In the pocket of the shirt that is all they have ever given her to wear she has crammed as much of the filth from the floor of my cell as she can carry—her gift to me. The room smells no sweeter after she is gone: it howls with its stench and my loss.

There is no time, any longer. There is only the mire in which they leave me, alone—except for one random playfulness, when I have bothered them with my calling for the rags with which I try to clean a portion of my louse-loved body. They say they will do better—they will let me have a bath.

In a room so abrasive with light it scrapes the black lining of my skull they push my head down into a barrel full of brackish water. I feel the stubby fingers, the calluses on their palms, pushing, as my head fights up and the white under my eyelids bruises purple, black and I am drowning till they jerk my head up, slap it back and forth to shake off the foul water that clots it, limp like a mop that has been doused in a pail of slime. There is no time, anymore, just the first time and then they may bathe me, drown me in that barrel once or a thousand times more. The only time that matters is the never I have lost: that I will never not have had this done to me.

They come like telegrams you are terrified to open: voices tapping through the walls. Always news of movement in and loading out. Sometimes, with a hopefulness so disciplined, so sober, it seems like a scientist's grudging acknowledgement of some miraculous cure, some unknown element, you hear and pass on news that someone among us has been transferred to the hospital; has been washed and cleanly dressed, fed on milk and bread and iron tablets till whatever slashes and burns that can heal have disappeared. Has been released into some far country that knows nothing of what goes on here; which may perhaps read of our disappearances in the back pages of shiny-covered magazines, or even see a grainy image of the mothers, husbands, wives who wait with an incalculable fatality for the fat men in mud-coloured uniforms, the no-faced men with sunglasses and black moustaches and metallic rainbows on their chests to come out and shake their fists at them from marble balconies.
  Such news comes so rarely that it marks the delayed death of this imprisonment the way a great catastrophe— earthquake, famine, flood—would mark the lifetime of some survivor, outside. Most of us who are here so long do not yet stay long enough to hear with our own ears, pass on with our own voices, the happening of such miracles: we only know they have come about, the way a child supposes that once there must really have been the castles, maidens,

witches, princely rescuers outside the paper forests of their fairy-tales. Yet I have found it better not to tell myself such stories, not to want to be told them. Instead I lodge in the black air of my cell, hoping for no-one and nothing; receiving messages of movement in and loading out, and passing them along: someone who has disappeared and thus from whom everyone and everything has also had to disappear.

For no reason, the door of my cell opens—is not pried to make the crack through which a dish or metal cup is shoved, but is flung wide. Two guards, with rifles and hip knives and bullet necklaces around their chests, have come to take me for a walk. Because I have been confined to a cell almost no longer than the length of my body, I am unable to conceive of, let alone walk down, a corridor as long as the tramp of their boots has made it sound. They hoist me up by elbows whose sharpness I pray feeds like maggots on the cushions of their palms.

I am pulled out into air and light and casual, unmeaning noise. For a moment every muscle and hair left to my body contracts, bracing itself for shock to the tenderest, most private and insistently camouflaged part of me. Not eyes or genitals or nipples, but the knowledge I possess, even if I don't believe, that one of all of us, one of the thousand still alive in this place, will be let out: made free. Stupidly, by some intractable reflex, the blades of my elbows pull back from my guards' hands: I do not wish to cause pain to those who are leading me to the door through which I will see my husband, my daughter waiting to take me with them, home. The guards tighten their grip—they do not understand.

They do not matter, nothing matters, I am in a blaze of joy as if I were some long-abandoned house whose rotten beams fire consumes with one fierce, jabbing tongue. All will be well, is well, has been well: I will see them now, they will take me out, there is only the end of this corridor to reach. This corridor and then another, and another: narrow, long, obliquely angled, endless.

Yet at last we stop. There is a door in the passageway; it opens onto another corridor that has a rough wooden gate at its extremity—the gate of a barn, or a garage. One of the guards kicks with his boot at the wood. I am in agony to which no torture has accustomed me—I can smell, through the slats of the wood, fresh air—air that comes straight from the stars, cold and clear and free of any human voice or touch. He kicks only once at the door—I would have him smash it with his rifle butt, bludgeon it the way he has so many skulls and groins—but he kicks once, indolently, waits, seems as if he would like to light up a cigarette if only he did not hold my elbow in his hand. I cannot even shut my eyes to help myself, I stare at the door as slowly the bolts are slid across outside, as slowly a free space is conjured before me. And then I am walking out, I am being pushed along a path bordered by barbed wire. I am being walked beside a pen, barbed also, in which is waiting, but not for me, my daughter.

They pose me against the wire long enough for me to see her, to know that the dress she wears is not one I have given her, that she wears her hair in a strange way that changes the face I remember as hers. And that she could never know this skeleton bandaged in flesh on which her eyes rest as fleetingly as they would on a dead and rotting crow, to be her mother. It is almost a mercy. She looks sleepy, puzzled, cross; one of the children crammed behind her treads on her heel, dislodging her shoe, and I know if she had room to move she would whirl round and hit at him. I think I know she would do this. It is so sweet for me to stand and look and neither remember nor forget but only see her—such sweet atrocity. But they shove their guns at me, drag me back while I twist my head to keep looking at her; prop me before the barn door they are unbolting, what I think is the barn door—but that has been left long behind us—it is the door of my cell, again.

I have had the most extraordinary dream—the kind of dream that takes you by the hand through numberless light, airy rooms of a house where once you lived in certain happiness, almost forever. Only to halt, and for no reason, hurl you out sleep's door onto that narrow ledge between night and morning, that blessed space in which you can feel, see, hear nothing to tell whether you are safe asleep or prisoned still inside your waking. Where waking is a belly-crawl over split metal, shattered glass; where sleeping is to find yourself washed after shipwreck to a welcome, opalescent emptiness of shore.

In my dream I wake from soft, dark sleep to listen for the echoes of some danger that has roused me. Our daughter has fallen out of bed and hurt herself; she cries to be comforted. Slowly I lumber out of bed, pad along the corridor to her room. She is not hurt, only sleepy, puzzled, cross with what is unexpected and uncomfortable. In my dream I pick her up, hold her in my arms, for a moment, before laying her back into the bed. She leaps after her sleep as if it were some beautiful bright ball she were chasing on a beach where there is pale sand and no rocks; in a meadow without snakes or electric fences. I want to stay and stroke her hair as she sleeps, but I know I will only be holding her back from where she runs to. And there is no need—she will come to my bed to wake us in the morning. She sleeps, and I take myself back along the corridor, into the room where my husband lies.

From our bed I can see the moon disentangling itself from the mazy branches of a tree. Slowly it floats upward, lucent, buoyant in its liberty. I put my hands over my own fullness and feel the baby, turning over in its blood-rich, blood-safe sleep. In a month it will be born, will sail on the flood of its ruined shelter, washing up on this shore outside, to light and air and cradling touch. In this dream, I turn heavily on my side and press into the empty space against my husband's chest. Perfectly we fit together, gently we touch each other. The house, the street, the city and the earth on which they crouch, all hold us carefully. We fit so perfectly, in our sleep.

Mrs. Putnam at the Planetarium

Tuesdays Mrs. Putnam locked her flat, walked three city blocks to the subway; passed, with the sombre airiness of a ghost, through grilles and spokes and greedy-mouthed machines, and rode from Jane and Bloor to Museum. Rode in summer, when the cars were full of tourists with cameras clotting their necks and the pale yellow tiles made the station seem a morgue, ice under the hammer heat of asphalt overhead. Rode in winter when the closeness of the cars made Mrs. Putnam, in her Merino wool coat, her black mink toque, clammy, dizzy, ravaged like a book with pages razored out. Did not ride in spring and autumn since those flighty seasons no longer existed for her now. Once there had been day trips to Niagara-on-the-Lake in Tulip Time, or Autumn Splendour in Muskoka with the boarders from St. Radigonde's or, more rarely, much more rarely, outings with Adam to the Island in late May, early September. Long before there'd even been a Planetarium, back when the Museum walls had been the colour of greased soot, and stone lions snarled in the Tomb Garden.

On this Tuesday—mid-November, snowless, skyless— Mrs. Putnam claimed the seat reserved for veterans, pregnant women and old-age pensioners and started for the Planetarium. Across the aisle from her were advertisements for office temps, notices for putting your newborn through university and pamphlets about Careers without College. Mrs. Putnam glued milky brown eyes to them. For the past ten years she had been retired on a pension sufficient for her to maintain her flat, though not to repair the cracks in the plaster or buy poison enough to terminate the roaches. She had neither nieces nor nephews with babies requiring to be sent to Victoria or Trinity College, and since she'd come by her post as English Mistress and later Language Specialist with only a Grade 13 Diploma from Harbord Collegiate Mrs. Putnam had no need to consult pamphlets at all. Yet it was imperative to do so—otherwise she would have had to look upon her fellow travellers, and Mrs. Putnam had no interest in anybody else's story but her own.

Twelve year olds with pink or green or orange hair, Jamaicans looking resolutely uncolourful in raincoats, Lebanese waiters mournful as blank television screens, Pakistanis with babies on their laps, babies with perfectly round faces and eyes like black moons in the dank heat or chill of the subway car. Arms sweating, legs jolting, Mrs. Putnam holding tight and tighter to the silver pole in front of doors out which her stop would show as welcome as the ram to Abraham, and in another sort of thicket altogether.

Changing trains she noted men at the newspaper kiosks who reminded her of Adam—no similarity whatsoever in colour of hair or lack of it, no slightest resemblance in build or height, but perhaps the cut of the overcoat, the precise indentation of the fedora. She was not the sort who would have held a lover's hand or gazed into his eyes, but often after he had left her side and was safely showering she would take up his hat from her dresser and press her fingertips along the crease his own had made in the felt. His wife had the vexing habit of presenting him with a new fedora every Christmas. She ordered them by telephone from Creeds; it was one of the few things she could do for him. The little else she could do Althea had told while waiting in Mrs. Putnam's office one rainy Sunday afternoon for Uncle Adam to take her to tea with Aunt Rosamund.

"She's awfully pale, of course, being an invalid, but it's amazing how strong her hands are—she does yards of crochet and knits scarves and vests and things, none of which Uncle Adam can wear, since he's allergic to wool *(though he wore cashmere mufflers and Harris tweeds, as Mrs. Putnam could have told her)* but he does have his office filled with crocheted doilies and coasters everywhere, even under the secretary's typewriter, which shows how devoted they are to one another. Aunt Rosamund's made me all kinds of tablecloths and comforters for my own hope chest—she says I'm like a daughter to her, since she hasn't any children of her own, which is sad, don't you think Mrs. Putnam? Maybe you feel the same—I mean, having no children, not even a husband even. I mean, of course you did have a husband once, at least you *say* you did, I mean—no offence Mrs. Putnam—"

Mrs. Putnam took none. Pimply, placid Althea, who hadn't the imagination of a pincushion and thus, any notion of the fact that while Aunt Rosamund was crocheting quiet mounds of doilies, Uncle Adam was taking more than tea with Hilary Putnam. Althea, thick as three planks, who couldn't recite a line of poetry to save her soul *(a soul the colour and consistency of clotted cream, thought Mrs. Putnam)* but who nevertheless passed all of Mrs. Putnam's classes for the six years she was at St. Radigonde's and her uncle at Mrs. Putnam's. Tuesday and Thursday evenings, from six to ten, and, perhaps half a dozen times a year, an entire Saturday or Sunday when Rosamund could be persuaded there was pressing work to be done at the Trust Company of which her husband was vice-president. Kind Althea, who hadn't meant anything by her remarks, since she hadn't the intelligence to think ill of anyone's peculiarities, but who merely parroted schoolgirl gossip about the English Mistress' marriage, which, as Mrs. Putnam knew extremely well, all the girls and over half the staff believed to be a harmless fiction, if not an outright lie.

Southbound to Museum Mrs. Putnam stared at her reflection in the window as the train racketed through a tunnel. The mink toque had been a present from Adam, the last she'd ever had from him. The first had been a ring—one topaz in a (twelve carat) band. To match her eyes, he'd said —and her hair, which was a watered blond, definitely not 22 carat, but then, all her own at least, and hadn't it made the first grey hair scarcely noticeable? Though he'd not been there to notice anything the night that Mrs. Putnam's mirror finally ambushed her. A massive coronary at his desk, or so Althea had announced the day after the funeral to which, of course, his niece's English teacher had not been summoned. Rosamund—Rosamund was still sipping the small beer of invalid life in Rosedale, having, to counterbalance her fringed nerves, an amazingly strong heart. Althea had vouched for it—of all her former pupils, Althea was the only one who still sent Christmas cards to Mrs. Putnam, rang her up on shopping trips to town, and never sounded disconcerted by the minute and peculiar questions put to her—not on the subjects of how many children she had, and of which sex, but of whether there had been any change in her aunt's condition. There never was.

Mrs. Putnam's was a different case. She had been a carelessly handsome, strong-blooded young woman and it had been to her the strictest form of punishment to watch as, year by year, the slow blue veins that Adam had once traced along her arms and breasts struggled up to the very surface of her skin like drowning swimmers. Liver spots over her hands, the peevish slouch of skin, cracks in her lips which, in the caustic light over the bathroom mirror, seemed to be fissures or crevasses down which her very soul might slip— these were to Mrs. Putnam stages of a cross made of real and not symbolic wood; they left scars and splinters in her shoulders. Her colleagues at St. Radigonde's would not have noticed—she had no friends among them and no confidantes; they, for their part, regarded her merely as an English Mistress renowned for the strict discipline she kept within her class, and for the tedium of the material she set her students. Not even Adam had known that, while she buried his niece under slabs of Pope and all of Milton's *Aereopagitica,* at home, alone, she'd finger a vellum Swinburne, recite from memory the lusher lyrics of Tennyson or read aloud from Keats in a special edition, gilt-edged with plump, fawn-coloured, soft suede covers.

Pigeons were wheeling over the Museum steps, or skittering after bits of popcorn that schoolchildren, on their way home from a session with dinosaurs or dusty Indians in the anthropologist's bargain basement, had bought from the Italian vendors. At their yellow-painted carts, crenellated with candy apples, fragrant with the steam from roasting chestnuts, Mrs. Putnam did not so much as glance—nor at the faces of the children, flushed against the chill of this grey air outside, sharp as icicles against their cheeks. Mrs. Putnam liked neither popcorn nor children overmuch—on the one she had lost a quarter of a tooth some twenty years ago; on the other she had wasted 40 years. In none of her students had she bred a love of Shelley, Scott or Swift, though she had done a creditable job in teaching them what sentence fragments, comma splices and malapropisms were. For, some fifteen years ago, the Headmistress of St. Radigonde's had decided that English Literature would have to be hatcheted and Contemporary Culture (plus remedial grammar) put in its place if the school were to hold its own against the more prestigious, if less venerable, private girls' schools in Toronto. Mrs. Putnam had lately read that no-one taught *Edwin Drood* or *Silas Marner* to schoolchildren these days— it was all Contemporary Song Lyrics and Shakespeare Comic Books. A colleague of hers, retired now from Weatherstone School, had got up a petition against it and asked Mrs. Putnam to sign, but she hadn't. *I do not care, I do not care,* was all that Mrs. Putnam had written in reply.

No-one asked Mrs. Putnam for the extravagant sum it cost to get a ticket to the Planetarium: on Tuesdays old-age pensioners were admitted free—into the Museum as well, though Mrs. Putnam refused to set so much as the toe of her ankle boots inside the place, now that they'd changed everything round and destroyed the garden. On Sunday afternoons after Adam's death Mrs. Putnam had walked under the arches and the stone lions, listening to snow or leaves fall as if they'd been the bells that had hung from the roofs of the tombs. Once a man not much older than herself had watched her from the window of the garden door and asked her, after she'd returned, to have tea with him downtown. From his accent she had diagnosed him as Eastern European, and refused, not out of loyalty to Adam's memory, but because she'd been raised in the belief that people whose names ended in *off* or *ski* or *vich* might be highschool janitors but hardly the social equals of a Stuart or Jones or Putnam— she'd had visions of the man stirring his tea with his index finger. Foreigners had been barred from St. Radigonde's since its founding by an interim Anglican bishop in 1833, though somewhere in the middle of Mrs. Putnam's term at the school *that* had changed as it had everywhere—Mrs. Putnam understood that the country's Prime Minister was married to an emigrant from that country whose flag looked like a checkerboard.

Once inside the Planetarium she walked up and down corridors painted the colour of milk frozen in the bottle, ignoring the displays of information on the walls and joining the small queue in front of the Projection Room. Waiting for the doors to open she looked down at her hands, then lifted them a little cautiously to her face, stroking her cheek with the leather, inhaling its rich, almost meaty scent. Real kid, none of that pigskin business—though she had to eat macaroni and skimp on the cheese four days a week, Mrs. Putnam would have her necessary luxuries, mere tokens of the things she could have had if Adam hadn't betrayed her at his desk that Tuesday morning, or, at the very least, if Rosamund's nerves had done her in before he had to die.

Particles of rouge like motes of rosy dust clung to Mrs. Putnam's gloves; all the heating and air-cleaning machines whirring through the foyer made her eyes feel papery, her skin crisp under the powder she had pressed on that morning. Why wouldn't they open the doors, why must they make her wait—70 years old and with the dignity, the presence of a dowager queen, yet they kept her in line as if she were queuing up for cigarettes at the five and ten. Where on earth was the Manager, he would have to be talked to, he would have to—. Someone in front of her began to whistle —further down the line she heard, distinctly, a belch. Mrs. Putnam drew tighter the collar of her good, her excellent cloth coat, pulled the mink toque down so it covered her ear lobes—shrivelled, hard now like dried apricots—and waited. If Adam had been with her, if ever he could have been with her.... But then, if there was anything she detested it was whining women, watering their tea with tears over the mistakes they'd made. *She* had made up her mind when she was thirteen—just after her mother had died—that she would marry well or never marry at all, having learned from her parents' case that life as or with a bank clerk was no great addendum to the sum of human happiness.

Adam had been charming to her—it hadn't been his fault that Rosamund had had the tenacity of a wire-haired terrier in her grip on life, on Adam, and on the president of Adam's company: Rosamund's father. And yet if desire, need and hope had anything to do with our lot on earth; if there were justice under the stars…. The subjunctive mood, Miss Putnam had drilled into her students' heads, is always used for things that one merely wishes or hypothesizes to be true.

But now it was as if the gates of a post-modernist heaven had been opened for the pensioners and straggling students. The inner doors of the Planetarium swung slowly apart and gathered them in like the great skirts of a Mater Misericordia. As quickly as her dignity and arthritic hip would let her, Mrs. Putnam found her customary seat, three rows back from the front, and at right angles from a certain twist in the crumpled metal that projected stars on the egg-shaped dome over her head. She drooped into the chair like a bird to its nest on a darkening winter afternoon; back she tilted, closing her eyes until her head had found its cradling place and the low music rising from the projector crept across her like a hand stroking her brow. And then she looked up at the great black bowl, not hard and blank as the subway window but soft, dewy, gelid—like a membrane to which Mrs. Putnam could raise up her hands, poking fingers through to touch the stars.

Lights dimmed, the music faded and a voice fountained from the projector, talking about Pole stars and Betelgeuse and Charles' Wain. The names didn't matter to Mrs. Putnam; she was lying in the grass on the Island with Adam— they had rented one of the small canoes and paddled out to the hand's breadth of land that was now a bird sanctuary; they had beached the canoe and were lying on their backs in wild, tall grass, watching the stars. For once he was not wearing his fedora; she had on her finger a ring with one diamond and a band of 24-carat gold. Rosamund was in Mt. Pleasant and even Althea had been sent back home to Thunder Bay, to parents who had at last decided that the advantages of a private education did not outweigh the loving kindness to be found only in the bosom of one's family. Softly Hilary opened lips that time had not so much as crumpled:

Now sleeps the crimson petal, now the white.... Now lies the earth all Danae to the stars....

and the stars sang back to her. They were not crystal splinters as children imagined them, but round, fragrant as waterlilies you might pick off the mirror of a lake and hold up to your face, breathing in their succulence and fragrance....

Across the table from her someone began to snore, with all the violence of a chain-saw massacre. It was hot in the darkened room, the leatherette under Mrs. Putnam's hands began to feel like fur and she was floating somewhere between floor and stars. The voice was talking now about satellites and lasers. Mrs. Putnam remembered hearing on the radio that before long man would be able to orbit messages in space—celestial billboards advertising Pepsi or the other Cola, *billets-doux* or messages of condolence that could circle earth forever, forcing their stories down peoples' very eyes. If it were possible, floating through a darkness cut to ribboned light—what would they say were she to chisel it into the night sky: *Rosamund, detested of Adam who loved Hilary alone,* Hilary who loved Keats and Tennyson and silk against her skin, and all the powders and perfumes of Araby she could not wear to St. Radigonde's, but which she would apply each evening upon coming home, whether Adam were coming or not, whether she believed in him or not, coming or going, leaving or loving, Betelgeuse and Charles' Wain, Miss or Mrs. Putnam, Althea and detested Rosamund and petalled stars in the night sky, looking down where she lay, in her story, nobody else's story—head lolling against the squashed leatherette as a voice explained the simulated stars shifting, blooming, exploding on the painted ceiling over the sleeping dark in which Mrs. Putnam lies curled tight, a newborn's fist around some fiction of a finger to grab onto, climbing steep, black spaces in between the stars.